# NOT EXACTLY a LOVE STORY

AUDREY COULOUMBIS

RANDOM HOUSE
NEW YORK

Text copyright © 2012 by Audrey Couloumbis
Jacket boy and girl silhouette copyright © Jacky Brown

Visit us on the Web! randomhouse.com/teens

Educators and librarians, for a variety of teaching tools,
visit us at RHTeachersLibrarians.com

*Library of Congress Cataloging-in-Publication Data*
Couloumbis, Audrey.
Not exactly a love story / Audrey Couloumbis. — 1st ed.
p. cm.
Summary: After his parents divorce, high school junior Vinnie Gold moves to Long Island with his mother and new stepfather and must negotiate a secret crush and a rather complicated connection with the popular girl next door.
ISBN 978-0-375-86783-5 (trade) — ISBN 978-0-375-96783-2 (lib. bdg.) —
ISBN 978-0-375-86606-7 (pbk.) — ISBN 978-0-375-89865-5 (ebook)
[1. Interpersonal relations—Fiction. 2. Moving, Household—Fiction. 3. High schools—Fiction. 4. Schools—Fiction. 5. Stepfathers—Fiction. 6. Divorce—Fiction.
7. Long Island (N.Y.)—Fiction.] I. Title.
PZ7.C8305Not 2012 [Fic]—dc22 2010048547

Printed in the United States of America

10 9 8 7 6 5 4 3 2 1

First Edition

*For Alix, who has never made it
a secret that she has a crush on Vinnie*

# ONE

On my fifteenth birthday, January 16, 1977, I slogged through a New York City rainstorm of hurricane proportions to buy the Sunday paper.

Actually, several newspapers, including those from Chicago and Houston. I didn't get the California papers. If I'd been born at the same moment on the West Coast, with the three-hour time difference, I'd have been born yesterday. Plus, the rain had already reduced the California paper to papier-mâché.

I'm a Capricorn, the sign represented by a goat with a fish's tail. Altogether, five horoscopes told me these things:

—I would suffer a disaster that would lead to a major discovery about myself. Good, with reservations.

1

—I would make a career move. We-ell.

—I would have an opportunity to see more of the country. Um, good.

—I would find romance. Good, but at the time, I felt I had romance. I decided this meant my interest would be reciprocated.

—I would learn that some kinds of long-term relationships are irreplaceable. My God. My *mom*. Or my dad? Maybe just a grandparent.

Just?

# TWO

My dog died.

I grant you, she was a pretty old dog. Her health had been poor for some time, and it came as no surprise when she just didn't wake up one morning. It's what old dogs do, after all. But that didn't make it any easier to accept.

Dad called the vet so we'd have someplace to take her. Mom went to work, worrying she'd be late, but Dad and I sort of took the day. We sat with my dog curled up between us on the couch, right where she'd died, and remembered all her best stuff.

On the way back home, Dad asked if I wanted another dog. I said no. She'd been my dog for fourteen years, she was irreplaceable.

\* \* \*

A few days later, I bought a Valentine's Day card for my girl—or at least the girl I'd been very fond of for two years—and slipped it into the vent in her locker. I signed it "Anonymous Admirer." I had an idea that would be more interesting than getting a signed card.

I'd planned to ask her to the movies or maybe a museum, and I'd say something witty about anonymous admirers so she'd know that card came from me. Mainly, I wanted to stand out a little from the crowd. I'd take her to a school dance for our second date, where I figured I would really shine.

She didn't show up for math class, and then she didn't show up in the cafeteria. Somebody told me she'd moved away over the weekend. Without saying a word to me. Not even good-bye.

Of course, it's true that I never told her that I thought of her as my girl. And she did leave several other admirers behind. I could see that she might not feel obligated.

Only a week later, my parents called me to the dining room table for a family conference. Not an unusual occurrence in itself. I'd been neglecting to take the garbage out. I had a pile of laundry in one corner of my room.

"Your dad and I—we have something sad to tell you. We've decided to divorce."

"Divorce?"

Dad's eyes looked like deep wounds in a quivering heart. Pleading for its life.

"We've grown apart," Mom said. "We're still very fond of each other, of course."

Tears filled Dad's eyes and shimmered there on the brink of his eyelashes, but he never let them trickle pathetically down his face.

"We know you're old enough to understand how this could happen," Mom said.

Dad nodded.

"The divorce will be amicable," Mom said. "We'll try to work things out so that your life changes as little as possible. In those interests, your dad will find another place to live as soon as he is able."

Dad nodded amicably.

Mom mumbled something about work to do and retired to the bedroom. Dad looked at me and I shrugged. A shrug that said I found all of this pretty awful but I was handling it. What good is it to be fifteen with everyone calling you a young man if you can't handle something?

I woke up the next morning to a case of galloping acne.

Yeah, yeah, I know. Everybody has a few pimples. A few pimples is what I went to bed with. By morning the number of blotches had doubled, and by the time I got home from school I had weeping pustular eruptions. That's what the dermatologist called them.

"Gold! What's happened to you?"

I shrugged.

He wore goggles and a surgical mask during the

appointment. If not for the rubber gloves, I'd've thought he was going snorkeling.

"Worst case I've ever seen," he said, looking like I might be contagious. He said he'd leave a prescription at the front desk and quickly left the exam room.

# THREE

Cultural differences. My mother told me this was the reason for the divorce. That's not to be read as religious differences. My dad grew up with a Hanukkah bush twinkling in the corner of the living room while the menorah was being lit, and baskets of chocolate from the Passover Bunny. As for Mom, the more candles, the better.

It can't be read as a personality conflict either. Having an insider's view of both a Jewish and an Italian family, I can reliably state that in the face of overwhelming happiness or unbearable sorrow, their reactions are clinically identical.

Further, my mother and father agree on all the important issues: which political candidate deserves their vote, child-rearing, women's rights, and whether the toilet paper sheets should come from under or over the top of the roll.

And they agreed on my name: Vincenzo. So what, you ask, would they find to fight about?

The root of all differences. Money.

Dad is an actor, and consequently doesn't make it very regularly. He took on the role of househusband. He's like Mary Poppins with a strong dose of that dog from Peter Pan, all wrapped up into one tall, thin, neurotic-looking individual in glasses that are too large for his face. But he doesn't have a neurotic bone in his body. He doesn't even have a lot of anger that his talent hasn't been recognized.

Mom breadwinningly brings home the bacon as a stock market consultant. She saw to it that I took swimming lessons Saturday mornings at the Lexington Avenue Y. That I wore braces when my front teeth wanted to overlap. That we all took ballroom dancing when the trend swept New York City, for Pete's sake!

Mom was behind this, I just knew it.

She dragged me along on a weekend shopping trip. My role: to carry the bags. "I've been thinking about you and Dad," I said as we crossed the street.

"I can't hear you over the traffic, Vinnie."

She stepped up her pace, and I matched my stride to hers.

"Dad doesn't seem to be into this divorce thing, Mom!" I shouted as she whipped through a revolving door. Mom shopped at the speed of light.

"It's upsetting him," I said a little too loudly as I saved our bags from the accelerating door, then hurried to catch up to her. It's embarrassing to lose track of your mother in a store at my age.

"Of course he's upset," she said, climbing the escalator like a flight of stairs. "I'm upset."

I saw that I was going about this all wrong. When I was a little kid, I got my finger pinched in a car door and the tip of it swelled to the size of a Ping-Pong ball. I was still blubbering about it when we got home an hour later, and when Dad asked what was wrong, Mom said I was "upset." It's better to appeal to Mom's softer side with logic.

"I know divorce is upsetting, Mom," I said. "My point is, Dad seems to be upset because he doesn't want one."

"I'm not asking for a divorce the way I'd ask for a microwave oven, Vinnie," Mom said, stepping up her speed a couple of notches as she headed across the floor. I hitched up the shopping bags and followed her at a dogtrot as she said, "I need to move on."

"Move on?" I figured she was trying to sound hip. "You want to live in Paris or Rome?"

"I'm saying I need to improve my life."

"We'll get you a Jacuzzi. How does divorce improve your life?"

She said, "I want to live my life, not just work my way through it. There's mystery out there, romance. I want to feel taken care of—"

Romance?

"Taken care of?" I cried as we hurtled through the cruise-wear department. "You mean by a man?" I said.

"Not *kept*, Vinnie," my mother said to me and to whomever else might be listening as she snatched outfits off the clearance rack. "Taken care of. There's a lot I've been missing."

"You're not going to get married to somebody else, right?"

"Being married is not my problem—"

This was good news. "I think you ought to talk this over with Dad. You don't need a divorce—"

"Let me decide what I need, please."

"All I'm saying—"

"Don't say any more." Mom disappeared into the fitting room.

# FOUR

I thought when a marriage was over it caused a kind of explosion. I expected a lot of yelling and door-slamming. Tears and recriminations. But all that really happened was, I stopped bringing friends home. I hung out a lot in front of the TV. Dad started looking for a regular job and an apartment.

Even as the days grew longer, the sunshine warmer, and everyone I looked at appeared to be walking with a lighter step, a sense of things coming to an end hung over us at home. We spoke in sober, hushed tones and acted way too considerate. Divorce was just the next step this family was taking.

I got home from school at the end of March to find Dad in the kitchen. This was usual enough—Mom wasn't much of a cook. Dad and I love cooking, and I always helped with dinner. But there weren't any onions frying, and there was

11

no smell of meat browning. No vegetables laid out on the counter. Not a good sign.

"Hi, Dad."

"'Lo, Vinnie." He was sort of hanging out in front of the refrigerator, whistling a shaky rendition of "Bridge Over Troubled Water." I got the feeling he was hiding.

My stomach started tying itself up in knots. "You always tell me not to stand in the refrigerator."

He shut the fridge. He'd been crying. "Dad—"

"It just hit me, I guess. Really hit me. I found a place."

I swallowed hard. He'd be living someplace else. I couldn't even imagine what that would be like for him.

He said, "It won't be so bad. I have roommates. And I got a job."

Roommates. Well, okay, at least he wouldn't be living alone. "What kind of job?"

"Taxi driver. I can work late afternoons and in the evenings, leave myself time to do rounds in the morning. A lot of actors drive taxis."

"I didn't know you could drive."

"Sure I can. But who needs to drive in New York?"

In a weird way, I could see this could be a good move for Dad. Not that I was enthusiastic about it. We ate cereal and left the bowls in the sink. I helped Dad pack his stuff and saw him off.

Mom was late getting home, and when she did, she seemed to have lost her footing. As if her new status loomed larger and somewhat too free for her tastes. Her discomfort was something I felt compelled to test. "So what kind of guy have you got in mind, Mom?"

"Don't start," she said. She was cleaning up the kitchen, something that was usually not on her radar.

"The professorial type," I suggested as she put an open box of uncooked rice into the fridge. "No, not enough income. An advertising executive, a little older, maybe, and moving in faster circles—"

"Vinnie, leave me alone." She wedged a tall cereal box into a cabinet full of pots and pans. "What time is it?" The batteries in the kitchen clock had been dead for days. "Do you have the time?"

My mother took a plane to Haiti. She was back in three days with a light tan, a supply of grass place mats, and a piece of official-looking paper that ended my parents' marriage.

Mom hooked up with a circle of girlfriends after she got home. Singles and divorcées. All of them compact—in build, in mannerism, in personality. No waste. Mom got stronger, sharper around the edges, humorless, even. It was scary.

Schedules and chores were printed on a chart that hung in the dining room over Dad's place now that Dad wasn't present to act as a receptacle for appointments, plans, requests, etceteras. After a couple of failed tests and then a warning note from my guidance counselor, Mom made me hit the books hard.

She was aiming for straight As. I was looking to pass. When third-quarter report cards came out, I stared at the print until it shimmered like water had spilled on the page. I had skated by with Bs and a C except for one real shocker.

Failing gym had never even occurred to me.

I couldn't seem to recover from one blow before another followed. No one tells you how things really are. Everything coming in waves, one rolling in after the other, and in case you're thinking that doesn't sound so bad, keep this in mind: that's how huge rocks, boulders, become sand on the beach.

# FIVE

Mom did the required school conference. She could say Mr. Buonofuoco's name with a straight face, despite the fact that I'd already told her he'd been dubbed Mr. Goodfuck. No one claimed to have any firsthand experience. His nickname was the student body's revenge for enduring his boot camp–level gym classes.

In class, I played it cool, saying to anyone who asked about it, "Good thing I don't plan to major in gym in college." Laughter all around. I didn't think it was funny. Or cool. I was flunking phys ed, *flunking gym!*

I had to talk to Dad about this. It was his busy time, the weekend. But I couldn't wait for our regular Tuesday-night supper. I was sitting with him about two hours later.

"Dad, can you afford this?" I asked as we parked ourselves

in an Italian pastry shop. A waitress came up to stand at Dad's elbow.

"Are you ready to order?" she asked. She was a knock-out, and I noticed Dad noticed. Big dark sparkling eyes in a pretty face, lush in all the places that counted. Classy-looking, too. A guy could wonder what she was doing waiting tables when Hollywood was only a few thousand miles away. We ordered cannoli.

"I can afford it, I just did a dog food commercial," Dad said when the waitress had gone. He looked a little embarrassed. "It's not a speaking part, the dog got that part."

I filled Dad in on the gym problem. He said I'd either have to be good at something athletic or be enthusiastically bad, but I'd pass fourth quarter if I was one of the two.

Feeling companionable in our failures, we both laughed.

Dad looked healthier, like he was enjoying life more. He'd never acted like a man who could make a living in the ordinary way, nine-to-fiving it, nose to the grindstone. So I didn't see him that way either. In the same way that I was convinced that Mom and I needed Dad's emotional support, I figured he would always be short of money. But he'd landed on his financial feet in only a few short weeks.

He liked driving the taxi. He worked the rush hour, he worked the airports, he worked the conventions and the trade shows. When he answered his phone, he quipped, "NYTD." He even got a couple of movie parts, actor-with-taxi. He'd grown into a success story.

When the waitress came back, she had mixed up our

order with another table's. She straightened things out pretty quickly, smiling and apologizing. Who could be upset with her, with those dimples? Not the men at the other table. Not us.

The weeping pustular eruptions took nearly three months to clear up. Most kids won't say anything about acne to your face, even at the cost of speaking to you. In a group they'll talk around you, over you, about you. You might as well be dead.

You don't realize the seriousness of your situation until some girl comes up to you in the hallway. The wrong girl. You don't look her in the eye. You strike a pose that suggests you're in a headlong rush to get someplace. This spares her feelings. And anyone passing you in the hall can see that you were moving right along when she buttonholed you.

When that doesn't work, you look her in the eye, trying not to see a constellation you might be tempted to stare at. But as she's telling you what an interesting science project you turned in, you notice how pretty she is. Really pretty. You notice her skin is clear.

She had terrible acne. Last year.

And then it hits you. Being approached by her means you've been accepted into the leper colony. The only kids who've noticed your acne has cleared up are your fellow sufferers. But she's still looking like she hasn't seen that you're poised to run. It doesn't help that you both know she's older than you and she's still interested.

That's when she mentions the junior dance.

# SIX

I went to the dance, even though my heart wasn't in it. This was another dance I could've taken my girl to. If she hadn't moved away. I know this sounds sappy as hell, but it's the kind of thing that goes through your head when you're taking the wrong girl to a dance.

She could dance, though. Because of those ballroom lessons, I'm some dancer myself, so I can tell you she was outstanding. She had probably devoted a lot of extra time to certain social graces in the hope of overcoming the acne lockout. I couldn't help it that I wasn't going to fall in love with her, but I knew I ought to like her more than I did.

Even though I spent a lot of time getting her sodas that she didn't drink—they're bad for your skin—she didn't drift away to talk to anyone else.

Once, standing in the soda line, I said to the guy I

thought she liked, "I'll bet she'd like for someone to dance with her. Besides me, I mean."

"Yeah. But I'd never do that," he said.

"Why not?"

"I hate when somebody comes up to my date and asks her to dance. I don't need that. Besides," he said, "she's too good a dancer."

It was downhill from there. She must've known I wasn't having such a good time, although I was as nice as I could be. We left maybe twenty minutes or so before the dance was supposed to be over.

"Usually this DJ goes on for an extra half hour or so," she said as I held her jacket for her.

"My mom asked me to be home a little early," I said.

I started for the exit, wearing this winning expression that I hoped would encourage her to feel we were both happy to be going. I hoped that would do it, because I didn't know if I could leave without her. She came along, sort of moving with the music, suggesting she still had a dance or two left in her.

"Hey, I think I knew somebody from your science club," I said. But she didn't know my girl very well. I think she was feeling mean when she said someone told her my girl had moved to Alaska.

She lived in one of those new high-rise buildings that boasts about half a dozen elevators. She said none were ever closer than the sixteenth floor. She only lived on the third floor and we'd do better taking the stairs.

On the second-floor landing, she complained about

something in her shoe. She slipped it off, leaning against my arm. She shook the shoe pretty good, but nothing fell out. "Do you feel anything?" she asked with a concerned frown, rubbing her finger over the innersole.

To tell you the truth, I wasn't bothered by any of this until I put my finger into her shoe. It was warm to the touch. I know it was only a shoe and of course it would be warm from her foot, but I didn't expect it. It was very personal in an odd sort of way.

The thing is, she was hoping I'd kiss her while she was leaning against me. It stretches credulity, I know, that she would want me to touch her warm shoe and somehow make the leap to a kiss. But it was in the air.

Only I didn't want to kiss her. Don't get me wrong. I wanted a girl to be leaning against me in this silly suggestive way. But she was the wrong girl. I passed her shoe back without any fanfare. "Whatever it was, it's gone."

She looked like she was going to cry.

When we reached her door, I wanted to say something to help. Like, *I felt like that at the beginning of the evening. In fact, I still feel that way, but I can't do a thing to help either one of us. We're the wrong two people standing here, and we both feel just miserable about it.* But I couldn't say that or anything else. Except that probably the junior class raked in a good penny to spend on the prom. Particularly at the soda line. Some line. And good night. And you're some dancer yourself.

Really.

'Night.

# SEVEN

If I had washed up on the shore after the dance, if the water had slowly receded, I could have dried my feet and gone on, maybe only a little the worse for wear. But unlike the dance, the gym problem went on and on, rising like a tide.

Mom's mood was excellent. Her horoscopes looked good lately. And she'd met another man. If he worked on Wall Street, I'd have understood it. But Mom and my gym teacher went to dinner one evening to discuss the possible reasons for my failure in gym class. Mr. B seemed sympathetic to our recent upheaval and open to discussion about my grade.

I worked harder at mastering gymnastics. They met again to discuss my sudden interest in gym class participation and yet again to celebrate my newfound powers on the parallel bars.

I'd had enough. Not only did I not understand why they

needed to get together so often, I just didn't like it. Then Mom dropped the cover of talking about my grades. She was dating him. I stopped going to class.

Frankly, it was a matter of some embarrassment to me. Not that Mr. B told any of the students, and I certainly didn't. But I didn't like the twinkle in my guidance counselor's eye when she asked me if I had anything new to report.

All through May and June, I shored myself up with the idea that I was only a few weeks from the end of the school year. Mom and Mr. B would forget about each other over the summer. Better yet, they could be over this little crush before then. I still didn't like it.

I liked it less when, on the last day of school, he proposed marriage. My whole body went clammy cold and goose-bumped when Mom told me. "You're kidding, right?"

A little smile turned up the corners of Mom's mouth. "He's a nice man, Vinnie."

"You haven't known him long enough to know how nice he is." They'd been dating for three and a half months, tops.

"I think I have," she said, almost coy. Definitely amused. "Really very nice. I think you're overreacting."

I'd had him for gym for four semesters.

"The man obsesses. He's compulsively neat, he watches football games from behind a chewed-up cigar, he's a coach!" Just so we get things straight here, he didn't smoke the cigar, he chewed it. Clearly, he'd never looked at one of those anti–chewing tobacco posters in the bio lab down the hall from the gym. The post-surgery victim of facial cancer before reconstructive work is begun. Very attractive.

Mom said, "He's more up-to-date than you'd guess. His mother meditates. She wears Earth shoes."

"You've met his mother?"

"Just for lunch."

Mom always said she made her biggest business decisions over lunch. She had me worried.

She didn't leap at Mr. B's proposal, but she said she would give it serious consideration. She'd divorced Dad because she didn't get to be a stay-at-home wife. Of course, now she was no longer a wife. One for Mr. B.

Dad called. I said, "Mom got a marriage proposal, Dad."

Silence. Tense silence. Then, "I guess she must be feeling pretty good about that."

Were they both reading manuals?

"I think it's pretty fast, myself."

"We're divorced, Vinnie."

"She still has a tan line where her wedding band used to be." An exaggeration, but still.

"You can't expect her not to see other men, Vinnie."

"I can expect her not to be engaged before a decent period of mourning is over, can't I?"

There was a telling silence. Then, "So, listen, how are your grades?"

"I flunked gym again."

\* \* \*

Mom continued to consider Mr. B's proposal through a few more candlelit dinner dates that she bragged about to her divorced girlfriends. I reminded Mom that she'd promised the divorce would not infringe on my way of life. I pointed to my grades as an indicator of my vulnerability.

Then Mr. B got a job offer from a high school on Long Island. He told Mom he'd spent five years in Forest Hills trying and failing to start a football team and, as luck would have it, this school boasted a fine team that now needed a coach.

He told me the school also boasted a swim team.

Okay, I swim. Just passably, not at all well. I don't really like swimming much. But what I said was, *I'm not exactly team material. I'm a loner.* It ticked Mom off that I said this, like I should want to pass the all-around good kid test or something.

She hadn't accepted his proposal. At least, she hadn't told me.

I think she let Mr. B take her house-hunting just to punish me. The trouble was, everything they looked at created in Mom a deep dissatisfaction with apartment living.

# EIGHT

I got mugged on the way home from the dermatologist. I was in the subway station, one of those underground mazes that run entrances over a three- or four-block span. At eight-thirty on a Monday evening, the nearest token window was unmanned and the station was all but deserted.

It wasn't a friendly give-me-everything-but-one-subway-token-that-you're-gonna-need mugging. He was too thin, like he hadn't had enough to eat for years. And shaky. Not like he was afraid of getting caught, but like he suffered from a debilitating disease.

He had eyes of that icy transparent blue, hardly any color at all. He looked weirded out. He gestured with the knife. "This all you got?"

"Yes." I knew I might be about to die. I felt a surge of

anger. I was a good eight or ten inches taller than the mugger. If it weren't for the knife, I could've taken his money from him.

He stared at the money. "Twelve dollars and forty-six cents?"

"I'm fifteen. What kind of money do you think I carry around?"

"Don't be a wise guy." The point of his knife dug into the soft skin under my chin.

I said nothing. A thin warmth trickled down my neck.

When I was little, I had a trick I used for bad times with my parents or teachers—anybody. I pictured them as animals. Mom or Dad as a trumpeting elephant, teachers as bumbling bees, clucking chickens—you get the idea. I tried, but nothing I came up with was derogatory, invalidating, or even harmless. Everything that came to mind either scratched, bit, or squeezed until it held a boneless rag.

"Look, you got all my money." My voice came out all quavery. "Why don't you just go before someone comes along?"

Mistake.

"You in a rush, baby face?" He leaned in closer. I couldn't get away from his breath. Like he'd been chewing crayons. Old, moldy crayons.

"I just think you're taking an awful chance," I whispered.

That's when a cop came down the stairs. He was still half a block away. The mugger was younger and faster, and despite being an unhealthy-looking specimen, he vaulted over the turnstile and ran for the lower level as I slid down the wall, my legs turned to rubber.

A train rumbled into the station, apparently on the other track, because the mugger came back up the stairs and ran down another flight before New York's Finest had even let himself through the turnstile.

The thing is, all the time I was sitting there, I kept thinking of how I'd handed over my money without a qualm. I'd pleaded with him to leave me alone, I made out I was concerned for his welfare.

I hated myself for being scared. I knew I would spend weeks trying to think of the snappy rejoinders I'd have come up with if I'd known a cop was about to come down the stairs.

By then I was crying. The policeman made me lie down, showing me where to press my thumb beneath my chin to stop the bleeding while he tried to get help with a walkie-talkie. We drew a small crowd, people who'd gotten off the train the mugger boarded.

The weight of this incident tipped the scale to Mr. B.

# NINE

Mom called Dad and told him she'd made up her mind. She was getting married and Mr. B was moving us out of the city as soon as they closed on a house. On *the* house. So if Dad wanted to get out of that fleabag hotel he lived in, he could have the apartment.

Hotel? Dad didn't have an apartment? Roommates?

As I listened wide-eyed, I saw the moment for pushing Mom's guilt buttons had been and gone. With the same speed and agility she displayed on a shopping trip, Mom rearranged all our lives with that single phone call.

I went to the library and got about a dozen books on self-defense. Since I wasn't likely to be carrying a cane or an umbrella most days, I leaned toward the books on karate and jujitsu. I watched a class, where it seemed people mainly learned how to be knocked to the floor. I went back to reading the books.

Mom and Mr. B set a date for the wedding, the day after the proposed closing date on the house they bought. Mom started working longer hours to pad her checking account. As a result, for three and four days at a stretch, I hardly saw her.

The plan: a weekend wedding at a nice B&B, and then we'd move into the new house too, just the three of us, the average little family. Very cozy.

As it worked out, the deal on the house fell through. Mom and Mr. B couldn't change their wedding date, but house-hunting began again, now with a kind of frenetic energy. I was drafted into looking at houses with Mr. B during the week, while Mom was at work.

It was kind of natural to expect me to go along with him, I guess, because we were both in the gym at the close of summer school every morning. But if Mr. B and I weren't enemies in gym class, we weren't buddies either. He had the class doing laps between volleyball games on ninety-degree days to build endurance. This was exactly what made him a target for unattractive nicknames. For the house-hunting project, Mr. B and I understood that we both had my mother's best interests at heart.

Mom took me shopping for the Long Island move. "Mom, I can do this on my own. What makes you think I need help?"

"The Island has a different look. You want to get it right."

"*You* want to get it right," I pointed out.

So we got basics, classic. Except for one sale item I couldn't resist. A pair of thin leather pants, glossy black. They looked good. They looked cool.

School started right after Labor Day, and we settled on three houses most likely to appeal to Mom. When he took her to look at them on the weekend before the wedding, she said yes to the one we liked best.

It would be a couple of months before we could move in. From the looks of things, I'd be starting at a new school around Thanksgiving, but I halfway hoped this deal would fall through too.

Nothing went wrong.

Mom looked happy at her wedding, pretty, and Mr. B looked like he'd won a really important game. The guest list was short. Mom's parents, Mr. B's mother, and me. Mr. B's mother was a shorter version of Mr. B, with only a little more hair, and I withheld the fact that she reminded me of a garden gnome.

Mr. B had started the job on Long Island. Between practices and evening games, he couldn't handle a commute, so he stayed in a room he rented near the school. Mom and I remained in the apartment.

He and Mom kept in touch with each other through chummy evening phone calls. They continued to "date."

But they had this comfortable way of being together, like an old married couple, the kind I saw on TV. They bickered as much as they shared stories and jokes, and it was a friendly bicker. A debate. They didn't have a mushy quality that would've embarrassed me.

I hated to admit it, but Mom seemed happier with Mr. B. She didn't hold herself so tightly, she had softened.

I had to accept defeat.

# TEN

We moved into the house on November 19, a date Mom's horoscope reported was a good day for a move. It was also a date that used to be my parents' anniversary. If Mom thought about the irony of it, if she noticed it at all, she didn't mention it to me.

As Mom had gone around the apartment taking watercolors off the walls, I learned they were hers. Hers, as in, she chose them, she paid for them, she got to keep them. It was surprising to me, I'd never thought of anything we had as other than "ours." The day was full of little revelations like that, and it left me feeling washed out.

At eight p.m. we ate tuna salad sandwiches, the three of us perched on boxes in the kitchen so Mom could admire the harvest-gold appliances. Personally, I couldn't get into the same light mood, but I got it that she was excited to be in the house.

Me, I missed Dad. More than when I was in Queens and he was only a short subway ride away. I wondered who would sympathize if I pinched my finger in a car door.

Mom exhausted the subject of the kitchen pretty quickly. She went on to say she'd change to her long-awaited part-time schedule this coming week so she could get us settled in. I could see she was also eager to settle into her part-time stay-at-home schedule. After the last few months of extra-long hours, I couldn't hold it against her.

Mr. B talked at length about a kid who had also moved here within the last couple of weeks, coming from a really good high school football team in Buffalo. He considered the kid to be some find.

When Mom admitted she was dating Mr. B, I could not understand how she could have outgrown Dad and then gravitated toward my gym teacher. After all, I'd figured Mr. B for one of those sports-brained guys who had season tickets to the games. But I knew him better now. He was a nice guy. Probably he pictured his football player and me being odd men out together until we found other friends.

"I think we ought to turn in early," Mr. B said. "Leave this unpacking for tomorrow. The boy's tired."

Somewhere along the line, I had become "the boy." At first this seemed to differentiate me from Mr. B's other students, but lately it was said with a degree of affection that I couldn't ignore. Mr. B was letting me and my mother know he saw us as a family. And yet he wasn't stepping on Dad's toes. This needed a delicate balance, and I was less and less surprised to find he knew it.

So far as school was concerned, I wasn't expecting much of a welcoming committee myself. I doubted many teachers were looking over my grades from last year and thinking *I* was a find. As for making friends, cliques would have formed. Maybe Mr. B was right. The football player and I might find we had something in common.

We might have to.

I went upstairs to my room and shoved a couple of boxes out of my way. I stood for a minute in the dark. The windows were still bare, and plenty of light came in from the street. Enough light anyway to sit down on my desk chair near the window and try to feel like I belonged there.

A telephone sat on my bedside table, one of the perks that came with my new position, stepson of Mr. B. It had an element of strangeness, like the plastic-wrapped sofa that stretched across the living room.

Otherwise, the furniture came from my room in the apartment I grew up in. It looked familiar, and yet changed here. Everything seemed to take up more space. As for me, I *needed* more space. I could feel an acne attack looming when a light came on in a room in the house next door. The light spilled onto the double-width driveway.

My brain cataloged this fact while at the same time I

watched a girl strip a sweater off over her head and throw it aside. She took up a position in front of a mirror and pulled her blond hair back into a ponytail, giving me a clear view of her in her bra.

I knew she was moving in real time, but I took everything in as if it was in slow motion. She appeared to be in a ballet of lifted arms and tossed sweater, her hair swung with a faint rebound, like the punctuation at the end of a sentence, the light reflecting off her skin so that she was almost outlined in a halo.

She might have been a painting done by an Old Master or, at the very least, starring in a shampoo commercial. This girl seared a forever-in-memory film short onto the movie screen of my blissed-out mind.

A woman, I was guessing her mother, came to her bedroom door and said something to her. It seemed, from the curt gestures of the mother, the toss of the ponytailed head, they were arguing. The girl swung open a closet door, grabbed a shirt off a hanger, and pulled it on, all while they continued a lively discussion.

They both left the room abruptly, leaving the light on. I went on sitting in the dark, thinking this girl next door was an excellent development. I wondered what her name was.

I heard footsteps on the stairs. Mom's quick steps.

"Vinnie, what are you doing, sitting here in the dark?"

"Deciding that I like my new room."

This wasn't an answer she expected. "I'm very happy to

hear it." She flipped on the light, making me glad the room across the driveway was empty. "Unpack whatever you're going to need for tomorrow. I'll make up your bed."

"I'll make my bed." I flicked the light switch off. "'Night, Mom."

# ELEVEN

It would be a short week, with school closed for Thanksgiving.

I decided to wear the leather pants on Monday to make a great first impression. And when school opened after the holiday, the ice would be broken.

At seven-thirty that morning it was an unseasonable seventy degrees. I'd never worn the leather pants before, and I found they worked like rubber sweatpants. I began to sweat, and they stuck to me like a second skin.

Half a dozen kids stood at the bus stop, including the foxy blonde from next door. She was not a disappointment up close. Swingy shoulder-length hair, shaggy bangs that gave huge gray-blue eyes a peekaboo·quality as she turned her head. Taller than most girls but shorter than I was, so maybe five foot eight or nine.

I like to think I would have smiled at her. But I'd just

become aware of one more disastrous side effect of the leather pants. I guess it had to do with the heat, the clinging, the rubbing as I walked. I couldn't do anything but cross my hands over the notebook I held in front of myself, down low.

I like to think she would've smiled back when I smiled at her. I do think she gave me a sort of once-over, the corner of her mouth pulled up to expose the dimple she had in one cheek. I hadn't seen that from across the driveway, and I had a thing for dimples.

When she offered up her slow-motion smile, an invitation to say hi, she offered it to someone else, a guy who came up to the group from the opposite direction. He was about my height, but with massive width and depth to his body. He was nearly as wide as he was tall.

As for me, there was an almost forgotten pull at my heart when I looked at her, and when I pointedly didn't, a kind of longing. I don't know if that's love. It's almost sad, that feeling. Excited and interested and hopeful and fearful.

I didn't speak to anyone that day.

I also missed gym class. With Mr. B. I'd left my shorts at home. I didn't do so much walking around between classes that I had a problem, and I was comfortable in the leather pants after that first experience. But I couldn't show up and run around the gym, shooting baskets.

I figured I'd explain all that to Mr. B later.

I hung out in the locker room. That was where I

overheard two huge guys—huge, as in not just tall but wide and deep as steers raised for beefsteak—talking about the blonde as they dressed for their next class. It didn't seem to bother them that they were running late.

One of them was the monster she smiled at at the bus stop that morning. I'd seen the ripple of expression pass across his low brow—he didn't want to look too eager. He smiled but let himself be distracted by someone else, and almost instantly, so did she. I didn't catch his name but in my mind it had one syllable, something with punch. Biff.

He put a textbook into the locker he'd chosen. "I got it from Melanie," he said with a moronic chuckle as he tossed a piece of paper into his locker. "It's Patsy's unlisted number."

Patsy. What a sweet name. It suited her slow smile. I couldn't picture *her* charging through a department store like a hunting dog.

"If she didn't give it to you," the other kid said, "what makes you think she's going to be so thrilled to hear from you?"

I was only watching from the corner of my eye, but I could see the monster was acting super casual. "I'm a hunk," he said with an expressive spread of his overdeveloped arms. "And I'm gonna be a football star."

I stopped idly spinning the dial on my combination lock. It had just hit me—this was Mr. B's *find*.

They passed me as they left. I must've looked like Gumby next to them. Especially the one who claimed to be a hunk.

He was a wall. A walking wall. I was grateful I didn't play football.

It was after they left that I spotted the piece of folded paper under the bench. The phone number was scribbled in pencil. It must have fallen out of his locker unnoticed while he was busy looking cool.

I could have put it through the vents in his locker, but I pocketed it. I imagined calling her. I thought about the dimple in her cheek, and about hearing that smile in her voice. I could say I was new in town. We could talk a little, discover we had a few things in common. Then I would say I'd seen her at the bus stop. I'd describe myself, she would remember me.

"You're that dork in the leather pants," Patsy would say.

And that would be that.

I didn't plan to ask her out. What would be the point? I didn't expect to use the number at all.

It was enough just to have it.

# TWELVE

Mr. B took it personally that I didn't go to gym class.

An emotional reaction, pure and simple. "How do you think that looks in the office?" he asked me.

By then I wished I'd talked to him before I went on to my next class, but I hadn't. That morning it hadn't seemed like such a big deal to cut a class, compared to the alternative. Especially Mr. B's class, because I thought I could count on him to understand.

Sitting at the dinner table with him and Mom, I got embarrassed. I couldn't bring myself to tell them what the problem had been. I should have been able to, but I just couldn't.

"You cut a class, it reflects on me," he said.

"I didn't mean anything by it."

"You think no one will notice it's my class and you're my wife's son? You think that doesn't hurt me?"

He pushed back his dinner of fish sticks, defrosted French fries, and canned corn. He went on and on about being the new teacher in school, and I could see his point.

I was the new kid in my classes, facing teachers who hadn't heard my name being bandied about the teachers' lounge over the last several years as an all-around good kid, bright, et cetera. If all these teachers had to go on for the first few months were my last semester's grades, and now Mr. B's reaction when someone mentioned my name, I was going to need the strength of a salmon swimming upstream.

"You think I don't want the people I work with to come around and say, 'Hey, Dom, the boy's all right'? That I want to start off telling *them* this isn't your usual behavior? Because I know that. I do."

The thing is, I never knew he worried so much about what people thought of him. "I'm sorry," I said for the third time. "It won't happen again."

Mom reached across the table and patted his hand. I didn't think it was a hand-pat of *Okay, settle down now*. She was more like, *I feel terrible it's my son who treated you this way*. It cut me to the quick.

I didn't think this qualified as a stab of jealousy, really, it's just that I was no less disappointed in the situation than Mr. B, and there was no one I could turn to who might squeeze my hand in sympathy.

Mom saw the cut class as an act of rebellion, not especially pure and not at all simple. "You won't forgive me, will you?" she said as she got up to clear the table.

Huh?

"Your father wasn't the one to say we'd grown apart and so he's the underdog, is that it?" I knew better than to suggest this was an overreaction. "I will always be in the wrong, I will always be the one you blame."

The dining room was set at a right angle to the kitchen, so Mr. B and I could hear everything she had to say from our seats at the table. And she had plenty to say.

"You have no right to treat me this way," Mom shouted back over her shoulder as something broke in the sink. "I've made sure you lacked for nothing and what do I get when I try to better our lives? The back of your hand, that's what!"

I disagreed. I thought I'd been about as cooperative as she could hope for. And it was about time she got around to noticing. I could tell her what really happened—there was that possibility—but where I was embarrassed before, now I got stubborn.

Mr. B tried to say a few soothing words. "Donna, the boy made a mis—"

"Take, take, take," Mom yelled as she came back into the dining room for the rest of the dishes. "That's all kids know. A little happiness is all I'm asking for, but do you think he'll allow me to have it?"

Mr. B glanced uncertainly in my direction as my mother ranted over the scrape of dishes and the racket of the silverware. "My own son, looking for ways to undermine my marriage—"

"Cripes," I said under my breath.

Mom tore into the dining room to wipe the table with broad swipes of the sponge that scattered crumbs to every corner of the room. But she didn't say anything—the silent treatment had begun. I knew the drill. I could get up and go to my room now. If Mom had anything she wanted to yell in my ear, she knew where to find me.

I looked back over my shoulder to see Mr. B hunched in his chair, and my heart went out to him. He had no way of knowing the mood was set for the whole evening now. And the way he looked right then, I didn't believe he would appreciate hearing it from me.

# THIRTEEN

The holidays were fractured.

I met Dad the Sunday after Thanksgiving and we went for a walk through Central Park. A movie was being made. The area was roped off and policed, so we mainly saw a lot of parked trucks and trailers.

For lunch, we ate turkey sandwiches with all the trimmings at the Stage Deli. Then he put me on the train for the Island and headed over to pick up a taxi. Ends of holidays mean big tips taking weekenders from the hotel to the airport.

In the middle of December, Mom put up a tree with different ornaments than we'd been using for years, and none of them were the ones I'd made. Dad kept those ornaments, but he hadn't put up the Hanukkah bush.

Dad asked some friends in to light the menorah, the

ones at loose ends because they hadn't flown back to families in other states for one reason or another. And on Christmas Day he held a potluck supper. Mom and Mr. B drove me into Queens in the afternoon.

I was lucky enough to get there in time to help with food. That had always been our tradition, me in the kitchen with Dad. With a stream of people coming in, we looked like one big happy family.

As we gathered around the dining table to fill plates, I noticed the apartment walls were surprisingly drab and dirty-looking. Dad hadn't done anything about the faint square patches where Mom took down her watercolors.

When I settled in a corner of the living room with a healthy stack of star-shaped cookies for dessert, Mona came over to me with cups of eggnog with brandy. "What is it, Vinnie?"

Mona was an actress and an old friend of both Mom and Dad. Also an acknowledged meddler, so I believed she'd agree with me when I said, "I just wish Dad would fix up the place a little bit. Maybe I ought to come in on a weekend, give him a hand hanging some posters."

"What for?" she said. "It isn't like his life is here anymore."

"What do you mean?"

"He's either driving or running all over the city to auditions. He's got a new agent, one who actually finds work for him. Sooner or later, he'll move on."

She was right. Dad was alone here, and he could do things that were all about what *he* needed now. "Great. Good for Dad." I wished I could sound a little more enthusiastic.

"Don't say anything about posters today," she said so that only we could hear. "He's making such an effort."

I agreed. Underneath the smiles and camaraderie, we'd all been making an effort. It was hard on the nerves.

I studied like a maniac over the rest of winter vacation. Partly it was that I didn't care to fall behind. But it also took my mind off things. Only Mr. B had failed to be impressed with my work ethic.

Mr. B being Mr. B, he encouraged me to go out for a team. Of course, he'd been encouraging me about twice weekly. When it snowed, he'd gotten all excited about cross-country skiing. I made a joke about taking up ballroom dancing again, but I felt bad right after. It made the man look sick and dizzy.

I kind of dragged around on New Year's Day, burned out on textbooks. I was thinking about how much life had changed in one short year. Actually, I said something like that to Mom and she laughed, saying I sounded like an old man.

She was charting her astrology, and pointed out that my sixteenth birthday was coming up. I said I was in the mood to do the kind of thing my grandparents did, where no one takes any particular notice as the day goes by.

What I wouldn't do, was not even tempted to do, was take Mom up on the offer to do a horoscope for me.

What I did, a few days after my birthday, was unfold that piece of paper and dial Patsy's number.

# FOURTEEN

I stood at my window and watched the snow fall. This was the third snowstorm we'd had since New Year's, fast storms that dumped a foot of snow that melted over the next couple of days.

I'd been trying to make the phone call since eight-thirty in the evening. Well, seven-thirty, but I spent an hour thinking it was too early to call. Stupid, because at eight-thirty I still had no idea what to say. I mean, I knew the words, *Do you want to go to a movie?* No—*Can I take you to a movie?*

Maybe I ought to ease into it, talk for a few minutes about something we both liked. Only we hadn't had any conversations at all, ever. I had no idea what she liked.

By ten o'clock I had planned twenty-three intros to asking Patsy to a movie. Sixteen were variations on *I have a question about the homework,* but we didn't have any classes together. The others were more *I'm calling because you interest me,* and I knew I couldn't carry that off.

The problem I'd been having, every morning for nearly two months now, we were both at the bus stop and she'd never looked the slightest bit interested in me. Which maybe didn't mean anything. She was always flanked by her intimidating girlfriends. What I kept in mind, her eyes were kind, I liked her, and I believed I'd like her even better once I got to know her. Now that I'd gotten this far, I had to call her. Even though it had somehow become nearly midnight. Or I'd never respect myself in the morning.

I reached for the phone. I didn't let myself think as I flattened the folded bit of paper with her number on it. And dialed. Put the receiver to my ear. One ring.

This was crazy. She was probably asleep already. I pushed the edge of my curtain aside for a peek. Her whole house was dark.

Two.

I squashed the urge to hang up.

Don't think.

Three.

Someone picked up, there was a rustling noise. My breath caught.

"Hello?" She sounded sleepy.

Air scraped through my throat.

"Who is this?" she asked. Answering her own question, she added, "A breather."

One panicked instant passed before I slammed the receiver down.

Breather?!

I was the kind of guy who calls and gets too nervous to say anything, so he hangs up! That was humiliating enough, even if I was the only one who knew. I had to be able to look myself in the eye, didn't I? But, a breather?

So. Do it again. This time, know what to say.

I could apologize right off the bat, say I'm sorry I woke her up, I suddenly realized I was calling way too late. I went crazy and hung up. And did she want to go to a movie with me?

Maybe it was an opener we could laugh about later. I picked up the phone again. My heart hammered wildly in my chest. Hadn't really stopped hammering. It was not a proud moment.

But also, I was absorbing how quick she was to accuse me before I had a chance to say a single word. Okay, I'd had the chance—I choked. But I thought she'd be nice. Now I wondered if calling back was a good idea.

I decided I'd give her another chance to be nice. I dialed, ignoring the way the receiver slipped in my sweaty hand.

Ringing.

It still bothered me, though. Maybe she wasn't the kind of girl I was looking for after all.

Two. I was tempted to hang up, I really was.

"You're a jerk, you know that?" Not sleepy now.

I hung up.

Okay, okay, maybe that was kind of jerky. But now—not once, but twice—I felt really stupid.

I also got mad. Some girls would've laughed it off or something. She could have been kind about it, that's all. I wanted to call back and tell her so.

Why not? It wasn't like she even knew who she was talking to. What if I was really just a confused caller dialing a wrong number? Only I already knew that wasn't why I was going to call back.

I tried to tell myself this call wouldn't be much different than calls I'd made when I was a whole lot younger. Rainy Saturday afternoons, two or three kids in a mood for mischief—"Have you got Olive Oyl in a bottle?"

The spirit of this call was entirely different.

"Boy, would I love to—" The sound of my voice hauled me back from the edge. There are names for those kind of prank calls. Callers. Okay, okay, I wouldn't do it. I could think about it, though. Thinking isn't doing. Except . . .

I knew what to say. I tried it out loud. "I just want to know, do blondes have more fun?" Yes! Ambiguous and obnoxious, a double threat. No tricky twists to trip up the tongue.

I grabbed the phone and dialed again.

She didn't pick up right after the first ring like I hoped she would. She didn't pick up on the second ring either. I stared at the clock radio, saw it blink from 11:59 to 12:00.

She picked up before the end of the third ring with an exaggerated "Helloooooh?"

"Wanna fuck?" *What?!*

"What?!" she said, echoing the word etched in my mind.

She didn't hang up right away. We had a moment of silence while I saw I'd gone wrong. Very wrong.

Then she hung up.

I had stopped breathing, and now I started to pant. I hung up the phone hard and started to bang my fist against my forehead. I felt like I was out of my mind.

Hold on, I said to myself. Maybe I wasn't so wrong. She'd been rude from the first awkward call, when she might have been halfway understanding. I couldn't have been the first idiot to throw myself, gasping, at the beachhead of her sneakers. This way she didn't feel entirely fawned over.

My breathing slowed to nearly normal. I mentally clapped myself on the back. Good going, Vinnie. The scared feeling of calling faded, leaving nothing in its place. Nothing, as in empty.

Which, when I thought about it, was scary in a different way.

# FIFTEEN

Monday was declared a snow day.

I followed Mr. B out to the garage, worrying I'd have to face Patsy, or worse, her dad. Mr. B and I shoveled our driveway, a guy with a plow on the front of his Jeep plowed theirs. I could swear no one opened a door over there all day.

It was just as well. I couldn't say anything to her, not after making that call. My intentions had been good, at least in the beginning. But things had gone badly. Very badly. It would have been nice to see her looking like she'd already forgotten it.

That evening, I called Dad to tell him I had a problem. I stuck to the story I'd prepared. "I got tongue-tied. Didn't say a word. And then I hung up. I did that three times. I feel really stupid."

"Not stupid. Just new to this," Dad said. "Rehearse. Until it's second nature, you know?"

Good advice.


At twenty minutes to midnight, I sat on the bed studying my face in the mirror. Still the basic stuff, reasonably well put together. A shadier cast to the eyes, eyes that hid a guilty secret. But I had a serious conversation in mind. I had written out what I needed to say so I wouldn't mess up. I wasn't feeling quite as nervous as the night before. I practiced my lines.

11:50. Ten minutes to go. I had a sudden picture of Patsy waking in the darkness and, after my phone call, seeing my light. I played the movie in my head to an unfortunate ending. I switched the light off and sat in the green glow of the alarm clock. 11:54.

A minute later, I got under the blanket and lay there, watching the clock. Maybe calling back right at 12:00 was stupid. She'd guess it was the same caller. Why answer?

On the other hand, everybody answers their phone at 12:00. It could be an emergency.

Or—She'd know who was calling. It was sort of an introduction. I'd apologize right off so I could get it in before she hung up. Maybe she wouldn't hang up. Maybe she'd be so impressed that I'd called back to apologize that she'd want to reciprocate in some way. Be forgiving, for instance.

11:59. In the darkness, the receiver was warm and damp in my hand and smelled slightly of new plastic.

12:00. I dialed. Leaned against the headboard.

Ringing.

Twice.

"Hello?" Voice sleepy but suspicious.

"I called to apologize for saying that to you last night."

"Is this a joke?"

"I never made that kind of call before. I swear. I'm really sorry."

"You're really nuts."

"I made a mistake, that's all."

"Tell it to the judge." Click.

I sat up in the darkness, my mouth dry. I'd heard the phone company had ways to track calls for the police department. Somewhere, somebody already knew who I was. I was breathing hard.

I started to pace my room.

She was just trying to scare me. "Tell it to the judge." A figure of speech, that's what it was. All it was. I sat down on my bed again.

My heart was still beating too fast.

In the cold light of morning, the phone call seemed like a really stupid thing to have done. Even more stupid than the others.

I wondered if she might recognize my voice. Not likely. She'd have to have noticed my voice to know it anywhere, especially over the phone.

Patsy wasn't standing ankle-deep in slush at the bus stop

with everybody else. Her friends were there, complaining that their boots were too fashionable, water was seeping in around their toes. One of these was an earnest-looking stick of a girl named Melanie. And another girl whose name I still hadn't caught, she had the velvety brown bunny look of an Italian film star.

This had looked to me like an uneasy alliance of two beauties and a hanger-on, but over weeks I'd come to the conclusion that Melanie was brainy and sensitive. Still a mismatch, but not a hanger-on.

"She said she wasn't feeling so good last night." Melanie was always informed.

Brown Bunny said, "I wouldn't want to be sick today."

"I don't think she's desperately ill or anything," Melanie said.

"She didn't stay for the last practice, either" was the un-bunny-like warning. "This week we're supposed to be running plays with the other team."

Ah. The powder-puff game. It was a girls' football game, juniors against seniors, played to raise money for a dance. However seriously this game might be played elsewhere, at this school it was played for laughs. Mr. B told Mom and me that last year's plays had been done in ballet steps.

"Maybe she doesn't really want to play," Melanie said. "You guys get pretty rough."

"Yeah, she found out it takes more than being blond."

"I'm not always sure I like you," Melanie said.

Brown Bunny didn't flinch. "Ditto."

I hoped Melanie was right about the reason Patsy stayed home. Because it just that moment hit me, Patsy might never have gotten an obscene phone call before. It was an unlisted number and all.

I've seen in movies how some women take it personally. Like the caller might show up at their front door. Of course, in the movies, he usually does.

# SIXTEEN

she clearly hadn't missed the whole day. She was with her friends and took no notice of me.

"You didn't tell us," Brown Bunny said, "about this party you went to Saturday night."

"My best friend from elementary school still lives in Bayside. She called up all the kids who've moved away from the neighborhood. Had them come back for a kind of reunion."

The trick to listening in on a conversation is to look like you're so lost in thought, you're unaware of anyone around you. Spaced-out. In a cafeteria line, you can stare at the un-appetizing offerings.

"Everybody came. Even this kid whose parents always dressed him up for school? Those matching jeans-and-jacket

59

things somebody puts out for little kids. Teachers put him up front."

"So?" Brown Bunny prodded.

"He picked his nose. Whenever the teacher turned to write on the board, he picked his nose, and because he sat up front, everybody had to watch."

Melanie said, "So forgive him! He was a kid."

"He still picks his nose."

I sort of knew that was coming. But I also knew from a couple of Dad's friends, comedians, how hard it could be to tell a story the right way. I appreciated the way she led the story with the dressed-up kid and left the nose-picking for a punch line.

"He stands around like he's inspecting the drapes or something, with his back to the room. He thinks no one will notice."

"Pathetic," Brown Bunny said, disgusted.

"Maybe he has a medical problem," Melanie offered. I liked Melanie. I wasn't falling in love with her or anything, but she had heart.

"He didn't recognize me." Patsy's eyes flicked in my direction. I stared, glassy-eyed, off into the distance. "Isn't that weird?"

"You must've changed a lot," Melanie said.

"I got so bored," Patsy said. "Those kids are still wrapped up in the silly stuff that occupied their pea brains in second grade."

Melanie was on sure ground now. "You are awfully mature. Probably it's because your dad's a psychologist."

"Psychiatrist," Patsy said.

I wondered if she'd already told them about the call she got at midnight, if she'd overslept because she stayed awake afterward. But then it occurred to me that, compared to some poor guy who couldn't resist picking his nose in public, an obscene call might not be interesting enough to report.

I was still thinking things over at dinner that evening.

Mom said, "You're awfully quiet, Vinnie."

"I'm not very hungry."

"Do you feel like you're coming down with something?"

"I'm just not hungry."

"Make sure you dress warmly enough," she said, and paused before adding, "You were up late last night. Studying?"

"Mm-hmmmm." I began to eat.

Mr. B stared at his meal of knackwurst, box-mix potato casserole, and deli coleslaw. Being concerned for my health, Mom didn't notice that Mr. B had lost his appetite. I wished Dad was doing the cooking.

Mom said, "Don't get compulsive on me."

I finished chewing, then said, "Any average under ninety and you'll tell me I'm not working up to my full potential. So what's compulsive? Ninety-eight? Ninety-five?"

"Don't get wise with your mom," Mr. B growled, but his eyes didn't leave his plate. Neither did his fork.

"Clever. A clever boy." She turned to Mr. B. "He's not right somehow, Dom."

"He's not getting enough exercise," Mr. B said. This was the start of a refrain that I could just about set to music, I'd heard it so many times, at school and at home.

The trouble with Mr. B as a gym teacher was his conviction that football was an important sport, maybe more important than baseball since it had a longer history. This led to two assumptions that formed his approach to teaching. One, that if you were good at sports, you played football. Two, that if you played football, he could make you a better player. Anyone else was a hopeless case and need not apply.

Since I'd failed gym, you should be able to figure out which group I fell into. This was okay, I guess, while he was just my gym teacher. But now I didn't just have him for Tuesday and Thursday, second period, I had him for breakfast and dinner. Not that I hadn't come to realize he was a good guy. I knew that about him, I really did. So I guess the trouble with Mr. B as a stepdad was only that he was mine.

"You said you'd go out for something," he added.

"I'm thinking about it," I said. He gave me the look that meant he was about to assign laps. "I mean, I will! I'm just trying to think of something I'd stick with."

"Swimming," he said.

"That was sort of a kid thing with me," I said.

"Vinnie." This was Mom. "You and your dad were going to the Y on Saturdays last January."

"Yeah. Sort of a Dad thing too."

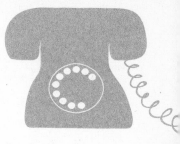

# SEVENTEEN

While I was setting the garbage cans on the curb that night, I saw Patsy's mom heading to her car. I messed around with the cans, hoping to time it so I could get back in the house while she was in the garage. Actually, I saw Patsy's mom pretty often, usually as we passed each other in the driveway, taking out the garbage. But tonight I didn't want to face her.

She looked like she was going somewhere for the evening. Then again, she usually looked like that. I started back up the driveway, keeping in the shadows, as she threw open the garage door.

As I reached the back door, she looked over the top of her car and called, "Would you set mine out?"

"Sure!" Sure. All-around nice guy that I am.

Patsy's father drove up about three minutes later, just after I'd finished with the garbage cans. He breezed by me at the curb, and I got a look at him as he stopped under the light at their side door.

It was the first time I'd seen him, and I can honestly say, if I'd been picking sympathetic ears to listen to my problems, he'd have been my last and most desperate choice. He had a face that looked like it was carved from a cold, hard material.

As I stepped into the kitchen, I pictured Biff facing the introduction and grinned. I imagined facing it myself and groaned.

"Did you say something, Vinnie?" Mom was reading her horoscope.

"Not me, Mom."


I wanted to forget the whole business. Just let it go, I said to myself about ten times in the hour before midnight. I couldn't do it. I pulled a T-shirt out of my top drawer. Even though that hanky business is movie stuff. No way it really disguises a voice.

Still . . .

I stretched the shirt over the mouthpiece.

Finger poised.

Midnight. Ringing. I just wanted to hear her say one thing: that she knew all along I didn't mean it. Well. Not that way.

I wanted her to know this wasn't the real me. I was embarrassed, that's the truth of the matter. Just thinking of how I'd acted made me cringe.

"Hello." Sleepy. And on guard.

"Please let me say this."

Silence.

"I need to tell you—" I stopped, hearing so much unexpected emotion in my voice. I lay back against the two pillows stacked against the headboard, the way I usually talked to Dad. I'd relax a little.

"What?"

"That I'm not what you think."

"You have a nasty mind, and you're developing a very nasty habit."

"I just didn't want you to be upset by my phone—"

Click.

"—call."

I hardly slept all night. She might know my voice when she heard it again. She might already have recognized me. If she did, she'd tell her parents this morning. Her dad could be over here any minute, yelling at my mom.

Maybe he'd call the police first. After all, it wasn't like I'd accidentally thrown a baseball through his window, barely a misdemeanor. I'd probably committed a felony.

I opened my door to hear part of a conversation going on below.

"—solution is a simple one, Dominic."

"If all I wanted was a housekeeper, I'd never have gone looking for a wife."

"Are you suggesting that—"

"No. Donna, don't make anything more out of what I

65

say than what I meant. I can screw things up enough on my own."

"Dom," Mom said, her tone softening immediately upon some sign of vulnerability in Mr. B.

"I love you, Donna. For more important reasons than your housekeeping."

"God knows you'd have to love me for more than that," Mom said with a laugh. She's a sucker for hearing someone loves her.

I shut my door again, very quietly.

Mom's enthusiasm for playing with her new house had lasted through the holidays. As soon as Mr. B and I put away the Christmas decorations, Mom apparently forgot where to find the vacuum cleaner. The thing is, I knew Mom was doing her best. She can map things out, but she needs more than cooperation, she needs a support system. She has that at work, she had that in Dad. I loved her, but it might turn out that with Mr. B, Mom had to sink or swim.

When I went downstairs ten minutes later, everything had cooled down. Mr. B had gone, Mom was just leaving. I made a bowl of cereal for myself. I squinted at the wall clock, the way we all did—the field of Italian sunflowers on the face nearly obscured the numbers—and began to breathe easy. No irate fathers had pounded on the door, there were no cops surrounding the house.

My breakfast went uninterrupted.

# EIGHTEEN

My second-period class filed out right alongside Patsy's.

"Hey, Patsy," the girl in front of me called out in a pretty voice with a strong Southern accent. She reached out for Patsy as she called her name, grasping Patsy's hand to give it a little squeeze.

What followed happened so quickly, I would've missed it if I blinked once. Patsy's immediate reaction was to return the hand thing, starting to smile, but she cut her own response short, the happy pink flush of her cheeks deepening to one of mild embarrassment.

"Sissy, I always mean to call—" Patsy said.

"I'm always busy anyway," the girl ahead of me said, sort of too cheerfully. "You know that."

"I know that," Patsy echoed in a dismal tone. "Do you

like your teachers this semester?" she said, mustering up a conversation.

"Oh, yeah. They're all real good about late homework and all."

"How are your brothers and sisters?"

"Oh, fine. Bobby Wayne'll be coming here next year."

Brown Bunny moved in from Patsy's other side just then. I had a feeling she'd been listening in from a few steps away. I didn't think Patsy saw her until then, either.

"Say hi to everybody for me," Patsy said quickly, stepping out of the loose formation of the line as she spoke.

A casual onlooker might think they'd spoken only in passing, the way Patsy handled herself. Sissy was in a couple of my classes, one of those serious kids teachers always seat squarely between two of the class loudmouths to tone things down. I'd never even heard her voice before.

I followed Patsy and Brown Bunny, something that was less conspicuous than it sounds. Students were shifting around, so all I had to do was look like part of any conversation if the girls noticed me.

"I didn't know you were so friendly with her," Brown Bunny said, letting her long teeth sink in.

Patsy said, "I was standing next to her, that's all."

"You had *something* to talk about," Brown Bunny said, cutting off that line of defense.

"I used to hang out with her now and then."

"Who?" Melanie said as she joined them.

"Sissy Donovan," Patsy said, her facial expression plainly

communicating severe pain. "Melanie and I both did, didn't we?"

"Hung out?" Melanie looked wary.

"Oh," Patsy said, with a dismissive lift of her hand.

"It was more a matter of carpooling," Melanie said, clearly irritated that her cover had been blown. "Our mothers arranged that, if you know what I mean. Before her mother died."

"That must be why she is so completely without style," Brown Bunny said, and it was hard to say whether she accepted the explanation or secretly reveled in her superiority. "Her hair looks like she cuts it herself."

"She's in charge of her brothers and sisters till her dad gets home from work," Patsy said. "She makes dinner for six people. And she gets decent grades, so she probably doesn't have much time for *style*."

"Oh, who really cares," Melanie said, and stalked away. I had the feeling she did care. And Patsy certainly did.

The bell rang, signaling the end of the fire drill.

I'd learned something about Patsy, the meaningful stuff of picking friends, and what we give up when we try to move up a level in popularity. If I was dating Patsy, this would be valuable. Of course, I wasn't dating Patsy and it wasn't likely I ever would be.

However, I was talking to her. Sort of.

12:00 a.m. and ringing.

"You again."

"Just hear what I've got to say," I began.

"I never heard of a creep who had this need to apologize."

"Exactly! I'm just a regular person."

"You sound weird. Like you have cotton balls in your mouth or something."

"I'm talking through a handkerchief." I didn't think that sounded as creepy as a T-shirt.

She said, "If you need me to forgive you, it's probably a sign that you're neurotic."

!!!

"What are you, a psychologist?"

"My dad's a psychiatrist."

"And you never tell him you're sorry."

"We were discussing your apologies, not mine."

"That's what *you* were discussing."

I'd hoped to get a laugh, but she said, "I probably know you. Why else would you care what I think of you?"

I tried to sound like someone who sat next to her at school. Somebody she knew. "I'm not a creep, okay? I do want you to know I'm sorry. If I wasn't, I'd be a whole lot worse than neurotic."

"You're going to get caught if you keep this up."

Maybe that was it—I had a compulsive desire to be discovered. The idea gave me the willies. But I said, "I'm not crazy, either."

She said, "*That* is what they all say," and hung up.

The terrible thing, I was disappointed when she did.

Also, I was a little offended. Her tone of voice had been . . . ripe. Ripe with being sure of who I was. Well, not *who* I was, but the kind of guy she thought I'd have to be.

Actually, it was just possible she was getting a kick out of these phone calls. Oh, not that she was loving them exactly. But I noticed she didn't hang up right away. She exchanged a few words with me, and when she had me where she wanted me, she hung up.

She must have been enjoying a certain sense of triumph when she hung up. Sadistic, that's what it was. It made me queasy to think about it.

# NINETEEN

in, veering around the room before getting in the cafeteria line just behind her. This was not an easy maneuver, I couldn't look like I was following her.

At fruit salad, somebody she knew stepped into the line.

"Hey, Patsy!"

"Daniel. Hi."

"I've been meaning to tell you," he said as if they were in the middle of a conversation, "I loved your essay on ballet camp." I knew the type immediately, just hearing his voice. Too thin, mostly nervous, always terribly precise when he's nervous.

"Thanks." Said with little enthusiasm as she chose a cottage cheese salad.

"Are you going again this summer?" he asked as the line shifted. He was riveted on her. Plus, he had a galloping case of dermatologist-treated acne, sunburned and peeling.

She said, "I don't know. I've sort of started thinking more seriously. I mean, ballet was never about a career for me."

"No? No, I—"

"Patsy," Melanie said, low and urgently, fitting herself into the space between Patsy and myself.

"Move aside, Twinkle-toes," Brown Bunny said as she horned in on Patsy's other side. Melanie looked hard at the food choices, and I couldn't quite read her expression—sad? mad?

Daniel moved up the line to pay for his lunch. Which is to say, he backed off without the obligatory adolescent male's repartee.

"He asked you for a date?" Brown Bunny asked Patsy.

I guessed "he" was not Daniel.

"Not the way you'd think," Patsy said, sounding reluctant. "Sunday dinner at his uncle's house."

"He didn't ask anybody out since he moved here, and now he's wild for you." Brown Bunny didn't sound happy about it.

"Please," Patsy said, as if this was a crazy exaggeration. But she was eating it up. She turned away to pay for her cottage cheese.

"I wonder why he didn't ask you to go to a movie."

Melanie said, "This is better, like—" This pause came

with a thoughtful frown. "Like, she's getting introduced to his family."

Brown Bunny looked skeptical. "This weekend, meet the uncle, next weekend, plan the wedding? I'm not getting the right vibes here."

"It's just a family meal," Patsy said, very cool. The truth, I think she wasn't too happy to hear that Brown Bunny wasn't going to drape a luckiest-girl-in-the-world banner over her shoulder.

"I just wonder who needs the uncle's permission, you or him." Brown Bunny had surprisingly good instincts. I liked that.

"You're making too much of this," Patsy said as Melanie paid for milk and a sandwich.

"I'll see you in class later," Brown Bunny said, which was as close as I'd ever heard her come to sounding like a friend.

I wandered through the maze of tables until Patsy and Melanie sat down. Then I chose a place right behind them. I heard Melanie say, "She's just mad he didn't ask her," and I let my chair scrape across the floor.

I was sharing the table with Daniel, who didn't even try to sit with them, although he knew Patsy well enough. He laid two textbooks on the table and set his lunch out on top of them like they were a place mat.

I could see he'd resigned himself to a certain position in life. As in, satellite spinning around the popular and beautiful, but never getting swept into the inner circle. I was pretty much a satellite myself. Just not resigned to it.

I had a book report to make up, so I started to reread *The Catcher in the Rye*. We never said a word to each other the whole period.

Mr. B came back to the house for a sandwich at four. Actually, I think he expected a cold dinner to be waiting for him, since this was one of Mom's at-home days. But she had gone out and hadn't gotten home yet.

He went right back out to run practice sessions for the powder-puff game. Mom came in about ten minutes later, carrying some Macy's shopping bags. Mr. B had cleaned up after himself, so she didn't know she'd missed an important pass.

She and I ate rotisserie chicken and potato salad from the deli. She studied her *Wall Street Journal*. I made notes for my book report. To my mind, Holden Caulfield wanted to get it together, wanted to be heroic in some way, but it was harder than it looked.

I wondered, was he Patsy's kind of guy?

I saw her going out as I was taking out the garbage. She was dressed in jeans, a fisherman's sweater, and a peacoat that she hadn't buttoned up. Maybe she wanted to look rugged, heading for the powder-puff practice session. She was getting into a beat-up Dodge with the Wall.

There you have it, I said to myself. Patsy's kind of guy.

# TWENTY

I didn't think I would call her again.

Seriously, I didn't. I like a girl with a sense of humor, and she hadn't shown me much of that. It looked like I wasn't her type either.

But I couldn't help myself. It was the song of the siren.

I dialed.

She picked up, asking, "If you feel so bad, why do you keep calling back?"

Talking to her was like talking to a debate team. I answered, "I don't regret these calls. I'm sorry about what I said. The first time."

"Still?"

"Still what?"

"Still sorry? I mean, most people don't feel sorry for what

they do for too long. They rationalize it, you know? Justify it. So the guilt fades."

She'd brought up a good point, and truthfully, I'd stopped feeling guilty. Now I wanted to feel, well, like someone who should never have felt guilty at all.

"Who gave you my number, anyway?"

"Someone dropped it," I said, relieved to have the conversation move in another direction. I fell back on my pillow.

"Come on."

"Swear. It was on a piece of paper, lying on the ground."

"Just a phone number?"

"And your name," I said. "Patsy."

"What's *your* name?"

I hesitated, then said, "Do you really think it's in my best interest to tell you?"

"I have to have something to call you. Besides creep."

I took a scolding tone. "Patsy, Patsy, Patsy."

"Got a crush on me? Do you write my name all over your notebook?"

I sat bolt upright in my bed. Her tone had changed, become so condescending.

"Lines and lines of it down the pages?"

Guys don't do that kind of thing. Okay, I was being teased, but not in a nice way.

"Mr. and Mrs. Patsy—"

My blood beat indignantly in my veins. What could

I say? I didn't do childish things. I made obscene phone calls.

"So you're not somebody who wants to date me. That's not it, right?"

"What would make you more appealing than the average Patsy?"

She made an annoyed sound with her tongue. "There's no such thing as an average Patsy," she said.

I grinned. "Sure there is. They have friends named Muffy and they date football players named Biff—"

"Nobody's named Biff."

"—and they wear pink with kelly green and they hide their ankles under little socks—"

"Why would they do that?"

"The socks?"

Silence.

"Because they have sturdy ankles that will thicken with middle age. If Biff sees—"

"Is this what you called for? To make fun of me?"

"I think we've already agreed on why I call."

"You're a pervert." It had a terrible sound, coming from her. Final.

"I'm sorry I made the crack about the socks."

"I didn't know perverts came in kids."

I laughed. The way I should have when she made that remark about writing her name over and over, like it had nothing to do with me. I felt suddenly that I was getting the hang of this, talking to her, joking with her.

"What's funny?"

"You make it sound like a size. Kids, medium, and dirty old man."

"Ha. Ha."

"Listen, I'm not a pervert."

"Did you or did you not make an obscene phone call?" she said.

"Yes."

"Who makes obscene phone calls?" she asked.

"Two kinds of people, apparently."

"Yeah?"

"Perverts," I said quietly. "And people who want something they can't have."

"And what do you want?"

"Think about it," I suggested. "And while you do, think about what you want. There are two of us having these lit—"

"You're obnoxious, you know that?"

"I thought I was neurotic."

It was only a second before she barked into my ear. "You know what else?"

"What?"

"I'll bet you're short!"

Click.

I guess I deserved that.

But as I hung up, I was annoyed with myself for apologizing. Not the first time. Just about the stupid socks. Couldn't she take a joke?

# TWENTY-ONE

"Don't forget, tonight's the powder-puff game," Mr. B said to Mom over breakfast. He had a bowl of instant oatmeal to fortify him for the day.

"I'll be there," Mom said cheerfully. This would be the first game she'd attended, largely because it wasn't a serious game. Actually, the season was over.

We'd missed most of the games through absenteeism, not moving into the house until late in November. Mom had used commuting as her excuse through December, I used makeup homework. I had a feeling we wouldn't get off so easily next year.

I saw Patsy throughout the day, in the halls on the way to classes and in the cafeteria. My luck that we didn't have any classes together, probably due to last year's bad grades.

I saw her come through the auditorium with another girl during study period, putting up posters for the Valentine's Day dance. I tried not to go around acting like she was invisible to me, but I couldn't let her catch me staring at her either. Especially now.

I was nearly the last one to get on the bus to go home. All the seats near Patsy were taken, if you counted the seat next to her, where she'd set her books down to save a place for someone.

I took a seat near the back. The Wall got the seat next to Patsy, and I spat mental spitballs at him for the rest of the trip.

Dad called that evening. I really needed his advice, but I wasn't ready to make a full confession.

While I was ruling out conversational topics, he asked, "How's your mom doing?" He meant to slip it in casually, just an ordinary family question. If it was so easy, I wished he'd just ask her. "I don't mean to pry, Vinnie," he said as the silence drew out. "I just wanted to hear her life is working out the way she wants it to."

I shrugged, even though he couldn't see that. "She goes to work. She comes home. She hangs around the house on her days off. That's what she wanted, isn't it?"

"Vinnie," Dad said. I was making him uncomfortable, sounding so bugged. "It's bad?"

"Mr. B isn't bad. Mom isn't bad, either. It's just not the same as coming home to you."

"Why haven't you said something before?"

"I don't know. It's just getting to me lately."

"Why don't you talk it over with your mom? I'll take a weekend off—".

"No, no. Easter vacation is only a couple of months away. I'll come in then to stay the week."

I didn't want to say that Mom had some things to sort out with Mr. B. It seemed strange to think of this as a responsibility I had, to hang around the house, but it felt like one. Not only because I had to live with Mr. B, but because Mom had to. I didn't want to be worried about her when I went off to college. I didn't want to worry about Mr. B, either.

I didn't want to say that to Dad. It left us with an odd silence that we didn't quite know what to do with. But Dad came through. "Hey, I'll come out tomorrow and we'll go pick up a tank."

We'd discovered a neat little aquarium shop at the mall. Forget "little." This store saw more action than the shoe department at Bloomingdale's. We had plans to buy a fifty-gallon tank and a setup. We'd had a great fish tank for years, most of my childhood. Up until I dropped a sun-dried sand dollar into the water, thinking it would look nice on the colored gravel.

The sand dollar introduced some kind of bacteria that killed the fish. It also ruined the pumps and filters, and we never could get the tank clean enough to support fish again.

We finally gave up. But after a stroll through that store, I'd gotten all charged up about trying again.

Plus, it could fill in for a required science project.

"That would be great." Not just the tank. Maybe I'd get up my nerve and tell him about Patsy. Maybe.

"Not too early," Dad said. "I'll be working late tonight. I'll pick up the taxi again at noon. Say one-thirty or so? Stop at a diner for something to eat after the mall."

"I'll be outside," I said, like it was just eagerness. Like I wasn't always outside waiting when he came by to pick me up. That way he didn't have to come inside, see Mom in her harvest-gold kitchen.

Patsy sat low in the bleachers with Biff, wearing her peacoat. I sat higher up, with Mom, where I had a good view. The game started off with ordinary plays, fuchsia pink versus purple, and the first couple of runs and pileups looked pretty serious.

The third play was interrupted by cancan music. The teams stopped running and started dancing. People in the stands—parents didn't know what the girls were up to this year?—sat surprised for a moment, then began to shout and clap. Patsy hopped around in her seat, amazingly uncool.

A moment later, the senior who carried the ball broke from the lines, making her run for a touchdown. In an instant the game resumed.

The cancan paused the game a couple of times more.

Then, during the downtime of the first penalty, boys broke out from behind the bleachers.

They were dressed as cheerleaders in short skirts and headgear that held little mop-like ponytails over their ears. The crowd roared as they executed a routine with surprising grace.

At halftime a small white poodle came scampering out onto the field, its sharp, high-pitched yapping carrying over the crowd.

A blonde came out next, a Monroe look-alike, okay, but also like Marilyn in the way she moved. She called in a barely heard but unhurried voice—unmistakably Marilyn's.

Five minutes of slapstick followed as the male cheerleaders tried to help grab the runaway. Marilyn tried to entice the dog back to her by squeaking a rubber toy. The dog wouldn't be captured.

Finally both ran off the field, Marilyn gimpily chasing the animal with one of her high heels held overhead. Belatedly, I looked down to catch Patsy's reaction, and saw she wasn't in place on the bleachers anymore.

Early in the fourth quarter, the juniors made a bold and successful move to take the ball. Parents stood up and cheered them on.

Right in the middle of the run, the poodle came back, Marilyn—Patsy!—coming along behind it. As the juniors' ambitious play went on, Marilyn and the dog continued up the sidelines.

The dog veered onto the field, and Marilyn changed

direction, running straight into the path of the oncoming teams. The dog escaped, but Patsy went down, with the players piling up on top of her.

It brought everyone in the stands to their feet. It brought me to mine. Was this even part of the plan?

The noise was incredible.

The dog ran up on top of the heaped players and down the other side, going to somebody on the bench with a dog whistle in her mouth. The players rolled away, picking themselves up. Marilyn also picked herself up. She smoothed her skirt, fluffed her hair, and strolled off the field. If it was theater, I could say she brought the house down. Even Mom was up on her feet, applauding and laughing until Patsy was out of sight.

The rest of the game was fast and furious, with seniors taking the last point they needed to win.

# TWENTY-TWO

11:58. I wondered if there'd be a coy invitation to say something nice about Patsy's performance at the game. If I still had a shot at convincing her I wasn't a fellow student. I wondered if I wanted to.

11:59. Countdown. Lights out. I rolled onto my side and dialed.

12:00. Ringing.

"Hello?"

"It's me."

"Like I wouldn't know," she said. I heard a little tapping sound, like a tiny woodpecker hammering away. Fingernail on the receiver, I guessed. "You saw the name Patsy and you called, not knowing if I'm ten years younger than you or ten years older?"

"Age isn't a relevant factor in an obscene phone call." I wanted to add *which I did not mean to make*.

"Just your first name. So I have something to call you."

"Pick any name you like."

"You know my name," she said in a wheedling tone.

She wasn't going to mention the game? Or the part she played? I didn't know why. Unless she was waiting to see if I'd bring it up. It was a little trap she'd laid for me. One that indicated she still wasn't sure I was a fellow student.

Should I admit to being there? Or keep her wondering. It would never have occurred to me to give an obscene caller credit for being smart, but they had to think fast.

"Probably it's not a very interesting name."

"Italian," I said.

"What?"

"My name is Italian." I punched the mattress. *What* a stupid thing to say.

"Are you serious?" And then, "It just doesn't fit the picture I have of you."

"Which is?"

"Um . . ."

"You might as well say it." I heard the irritation in my voice and I guess she did, too. She took a second to venture an answer.

"I thought maybe you're ugly."

"Ugly?"

"You could be. Why else would you call like this?"

I ignored that. "How does my name being Italian change things?"

"I guess . . . it's romantic. Italian. You know."

She was one crazy girl. I liked that. The sad truth was, I liked her. I said, "I've seen some ugly Italians in my time."

"Do you have any scars?"

"Scars?"

"If you aren't ugly but you don't want me to see you—"

"Cripes." She had some imagination.

"No scars," she concluded.

"No."

"So you didn't know it was me. The actual me, Patsy."

I laughed. Was I admitting I knew who she was all along? Was that wise?

"I guess I can understand it, anyway."

"How's that?"

"Oh, you know. I mean, I guess I can understand what you're feeling if you're just . . . ordinary."

She left me gasping. "Has it ever occurred to you that I might not make obscene phone calls out of total admiration? I mean, maybe I called you because you looked like you'd be receptive to—"

Click.

Sociologists have pointed out that attractive people get treated better than less-attractive ones. They get complimented more often. They get unsolicited favors. They get a distorted impression of their importance. It makes sense.

If you looked in a mirror and saw that you were beautiful, you'd be satisfied, wouldn't you? You'd look more often, and each time you'd feel that same satisfaction. After a while, you wouldn't have to look in the mirror to get that feeling going. You'd just have to think about it. Or not. Satisfaction with yourself is something that can get to be a habit.

Patsy found this phone-call business titillating not because I was attracted to her but because it was a different approach. The problem would soon be how to hold her interest.

# TWENTY-THREE

On Saturday morning, Mom made pancakes from an "add water only" mix and some kind of quickie frozen sausage. She was making a show of it, wearing an actual apron.

Despite the cardboard pancakes, Mr. B was in excellent spirits. He'd found a nice review of the game in the local paper and he didn't spare us any insider details he supposed we might have missed. It was nothing we hadn't gone over more enthusiastically after getting home the night before.

As for me, I was somewhat preoccupied. I had as much as admitted to Patsy that I knew who she was. The actual her. I could deny it again, of course, but did it matter? The main thing was not to be found out.

I poured more syrup over the cardboard pancakes. Big bites with lots of syrup was the definitive technique here.

Maybe Mr. B read our not-so-high-spirited responses as a sign that he might sound like he was bragging, because he added something that was news to me. "That girl next door came up with the whole skit herself. I didn't know half of what she had planned, just the other girls did. I never would have dared put her underneath a pileup."

Mom took a bite of her own pancake and chewed vigorously. "I think we should go out on Saturday mornings. Make a tradition of it," she said, taking up the horoscope page that Mr. B had set at her place.

"I have practice on Saturdays all through football season, don't forget," Mr. B said.

"You could take your thermos and a box of donuts out and watch practice from the bleachers, Mom." I chewed thoughtfully, if not enthusiastically, on as much pancake as I could wad onto my fork. "Or you could take a cooking class on Saturdays."

I avoided meeting their eyes during the brief silence that followed. "Vinnie?" Mom sounded like she was going to check my forehead for a fever.

"Just an idea," I said.


Dad was already waiting when I got outside. I took the passenger side of the front seat and he flipped the flag on the meter to start it working.

I was surprised. "You're paying for this trip?"

"Hey, it's not that big a deal. I had two fares to work my way out here. This way, my boss has no complaints."

"Before you drove a taxi, you hated for us to take one. You said they cost too much money."

"I've had a change of heart."

"Guess so."

"Tell me about your week," Dad said as we headed for the mall.

I told him I was feeling a certain amount of pressure to get involved in a team sport.

"Like soccer?" Dad asked. Neither one of us was crazy about soccer.

"More or less."

"What are your options for 'less'?"

"Basketball, maybe."

"I understand the school has a swim team."

Dad knows I don't like the water, but that never quite translates for him. He doesn't get it that it means I don't like swimming. There's a sensation in my chest from water pressure, a kind of weight settling over me. When I didn't reply, he came up with "Track?"

Track. That would never have occurred to me. "Is that a team sport?"

"I think the term 'track team' will stand you in good stead here."

We dropped the subject as we approached the mall. Traffic was heavy, but Dad was undaunted. He wove his way across the lanes with the aplomb of a man who won't have to pay for the auto-repair fees he incurs.

"You're quite a driver," I said.

"It's important to remember it's a team sport," Dad said as he slowed to let another driver into the stream of traffic. A few minutes later, he made a left turn into the mall parking lot.

I spotted Sissy behind the counter as we entered the aquarium store. I raised a hand. She nodded, accepted a charge card from a man in a suede shirt, and made herself busy, too busy to talk.

"Friend from school?"

"Not really. We have a couple classes together."

Sissy looked up at me once or twice as she packed all the guy's stuff into two cartons, smiling crookedly. Dad and I strolled around the shop.

Probably this was the perfect moment to open up a serious conversation about Patsy and the phone calls, but frankly, it wasn't the perfect place. Not only because it was a public place, but because it was too interesting.

The store featured a major floor-to-ceiling saltwater tank that held huge specimens. There was a mezzanine lit only by the light from the tanks. Most of the upstairs wall space was given over to fifty-gallon saltwater tanks. Dad and I wandered around up there for an hour before we settled on making up a list of what I would need.

We made decisions about air pumps and filters, and an assortment of other details. Some old guy was drafting arm-length sales slips while a couple of college kids ran around, getting the stuff the other customers were buying. By then, I think Sissy had forgotten I was there.

Dad got into line, saying, "Go do some thinking about fish."

We both already knew what fish and snails we'd buy to help keep the tank clean, and that I would start with a few angelfish as the main event. This was a generous offer to hang around in front of the tanks upstairs instead of waiting in line down below.

I also had an aerial view of Sissy, who was kept busy scraping out charge-card purchases on a little machine that was nailed to the counter. And of Patsy, as she came in. I moved a few feet to stand next to a murky hundred-gallon tank, the bottom of which was dense with natural seaweed.

I stood right above them. I was mostly hidden behind the seaweed, but I could hear the girls clearly. I could even see them, although a grouper passed back and forth at regular intervals, briefly blocking my view.

# TWENTY-FOUR

"Patsy," Sissy said. "Are you here to buy fish?"

"No," Patsy said, looking embarrassed. "I came to see you. I feel awful about the other day—"

"It doesn't matter. Really," Sissy said, looking apologetic. "I know how things are now." Then she turned away because Dad was handing over his card.

Patsy stood there for another thirty seconds or so, looking stricken, then left. I went downstairs to help Dad carry the equipment out without making eye contact with Sissy. I acted like I'd forgotten she was there.

Dad and I hit a diner for a three o'clock lunch, and then he drove me home. It was time for him to get back to work. So far as I could tell, he was happy when he was driving.

"Why didn't you ever do this before, Dad?"

"Drive a taxi?" He looked over at me. "Or you mean, get a regular job?"

I felt stupid. "I don't mean it like that, exactly. Just, this seems to suit you."

"We weren't short of money, Vinnie. And I thought your mother and I were all right. With everything. I liked being the one who stayed home. She liked that I was. Mostly."

Neither one of us said anything for a minute. I wanted to apologize, but that might have made it worse. I said, "You ought to put up some posters around the apartment, you know? Brighten it up."

"I'll help you carry the tank to the back door, Vinnie," Dad said, turning onto the block where I lived now.

"I've got it," I told him.

He stopped the taxi in front of the house. He helped me with the load, setting it onto the driveway while I trucked stuff to the door. When the trunk was empty, I said, "I'll donkey the rest of it."

Patsy came out then, wearing that peacoat again. She appeared to be surprised to see us outside. She gave us an uncertain smile and took off down the sidewalk, walking away with a brisk step.

"Friend of yours?" Dad asked.

"We ride the same bus." Impersonal, that's how I tried to sound. I don't know that I made it.

Dad clapped me on the arm. "Nice scenery you have in

this neighborhood." And he got into the taxi. When he was lucky, he picked up a fare for the trip back.

"Anthony!" she said, like she was greeting an old friend.

"Anthony?" It caught me by surprise. A point for her. "No?"

"No," I said, understanding. "And you mean Antonio."

"Maybe you're the wrong guy. You want to say something obscene?"

"I told you. That was a mistake."

"What does your dad do?"

Safe territory. "He's an actor."

"Yeah?"

"He's not famous. Mostly, he does commercials."

"Will I have seen any?"

"There's a dog food commercial running now." I wished I'd changed it to breakfast cereal, I look a lot like my dad.

"Tell me something else about yourself."

"I'm shy," I said.

"Uh-huh. Athletic?"

Careful here, I thought.

Remembering Mr. B's recent enthusiasm, I said, "Skiing."

"Skiing is sexy."

"Skiing is a one-way ticket to frostbite and a runny nose."

She laughed. "You're cute, Aldo."

"Now, *that* you can't be sure of. And one name per call."

"One letter per call, that's our rule. I can try as many names as I like."

*Our rule.* I liked the sound of that. "We'll see."

"Very in charge, are you?"

"I'm the only one with a number to call," I said.

"I think you're short *and* you have an inferiority complex, Andreo."

"Italian is not French with an *o* at the end."

"I bet you get good grades."

My gut tightened. "Sometimes."

"So you're in my classes?"

"Not."

"You're sure?"

"There must be dozens of guys in your classes. Why would I need to lie about that?"

No answer.

I breathed a little easier. I said, "Don't go away mad."

"I'm not going away."

"You always go away. I just have to say something dirty."

"So go ahead, say it."

I didn't speak.

"Say it!"

I whispered, "Filthy, filthy, filthy."

She hung up.

I laughed, I couldn't help it.

# TWENTY-FIVE

Late the next morning, Mom made scrambled eggs, then fried them, and finally tossed them into the wastebasket. She forgot to turn on the broiler, so the bacon didn't burn, but the toast did. This was the point at which Mr. B entered the kitchen, his hair still wet from the shower.

I pulled on a zippered sweatshirt, getting ready to go outside. Plucking the Sunday paper off the lawn was my small contribution to family harmony. "You can't go out like that again today, Vinnie," Mom said as she put some frozen sausages into the toaster oven with a couple more slices of bread. "Put on your heavier jacket."

"It looks warm out."

"The sun is shining. That doesn't make it warm out."

"I think that's how it works, Mom."

"Don't be smart. Was that you sneezing? Maybe you caught a cold."

I hated that jacket. It made me look like the puffy Michelin Man. I hoped the day would warm up, like it had the day before.

"A cold, maybe," she said, shaking the jar of vitamin C pills.

"Let the boy alone," Mr. B said, contemplating a cup of coffee he clearly didn't approve of. "I sneezed, and I don't have a cold either."

Mom playfully, but also meaningfully, clipped him on the shoulder. "I'll be the mother here."

"And I'll be the stepdad," Mr. B said with a grin as she set out an open box of donuts—plain, soft white sugar, and cinnamon. I grabbed one and dipped it into Mom's coffee.

"Vinnie will be the stepson," Mom said as Mr. B reached for a cinnamon donut. But mine fell apart before I could get it into my mouth, plopping with a wet smack onto the floor.

Stepson.

It was a word that came up with distressing frequency. Each time it did, my heart thudded to a halt. Mr. B and I would be sitting across from each other at breakfast and dinner for the next couple of years, maybe more. We'd spend holidays together, vacations, and even a Saturday-night movie here and there.

Today, for instance, Mr. B had a free day. Sunday at home. So when Mom asked him what he planned to do with it and he said he wanted to clean the kitchen, I said, "I'll help." Mom had already made plans to go into the city for an art show with one of those divorced girlfriends she used to hang out with. She gave us a horrified glance and took flight. "See you guys later!"

When I finally headed outside for the paper, I left the puffy jacket behind. I was glad I did. As I turned to come inside with the paper, Patsy stepped outside in a soft green skirt all full of folds, and a lacy blouse. Like something out of the pages of a magazine. She carried her coat over her arm. It was chilly enough for her to have worn the damn coat, but no doubt she didn't want to spoil the effect.

I strung out the walk up the driveway. A Lincoln pulled up in front of Patsy's house. She ran to the car and got in. I heard her talking happily before she slammed the door shut.

I figured the Wall got the old man's car.


I was assigned the refrigerator, while Mr. B took the enamel top off the stove and scrubbed it with a steel pad. I could see he was likely to go straight through the whole house this way.

The kitchen was only the tip of the iceberg. Mom didn't have Dad's touch with the house. Our bathtub drain was often clogged, creating a pool of marshy water. The dining room floor was sticky, and sneakers made a crickly noise as we crossed it. Dust lay in the corners of the dining room chairs because Mom dusted the way I used to do it. Dad always made me do it over.

This is going to sound funny, but I didn't mind that

Mr. B expected me to help, sharing a little elbow grease. We started to clear the kitchen counter, which immediately necessitated rearranging the cabinets above and below. I talked fish tanks and he talked food.

One thing I'd noticed about Mr. B—he was neat. No. He was meticulous. I wondered if Mom had ever noticed his office during those parent-teacher meetings last year. White gloves had nothing to fear.

I wondered if he ever mentioned to her that each of his gym classes this year have devoted two periods each to climbing over the lockers with a wet rag, cleaning off years of tarlike dust deposits and the occasional ragged sneaker or balled-up sock. We'd disinfected shower tiles. We'd wiped out our lockers only to have Mr. B point out the curled lips of metal inside the vented door as a dirt catcher. He planned to start on the gym supply closet next week.

The janitorial crew must love him.


Mr. B turned on the TV to watch televised reruns of famous games.

I set the fish tank in the living room, in front of a bank of three windows. I laid everything out on the floor around the tank—the air filter, the water pump, the heater, and the light—and started reading a variety of instruction booklets. It would be a couple of weeks before I'd be ready to put any fish into the tank. Maybe a month before I'd get the salt water just right.

It was good the windows happened to be on the north

side of the house. No sun to overheat the water. Also, while feeding the fish or cleaning the tank, I'd be able to watch the comings and goings over at Patsy's.

Mom came home carrying a small watercolor. She held it up for Mr. B and me, then spent about an hour walking it around the house, deciding where to hang it. During this time, Patsy's mother made the garbage trip. I looked up as I placed a crystal cave into the blue gravel. I smiled and waved, feeling very boy-next-door.

Mr. B asked, "What are we having for dinner, hon?"

"Dinner? Haven't you two eaten yet?"

Mr. B shook himself out of his sports daze. "Have you?"

"I grabbed something to nosh on the train," she said. "But I think there must be some eggs. Some breakfast links in the freezer, maybe?"

# TWENTY-SIX

The thing Patsy got me thinking about, once the lights were out and the dial tone *brrrrrred* in my ear, a kind of alter ego took over when I called her. It wasn't really me she was talking to. No. It was Vincenzo.

At first this felt kind of scary. But the more I thought about it, the better the whole idea looked to me. I couldn't be held responsible for anything Vincenzo said. And Vincenzo could say—well, anything.

Besides, he only existed for ten or fifteen minutes a day.

At midnight Patsy picked up, opening the conversation with a question. "Have you ever had a girlfriend, Bernardo?"

"Of course I have." I chuckled. I hated myself immediately.

"Do you have one now?"

"Are you asking, am I cheating on her?"

Silence.

"Currently, I'm only seeing you," I said. "In a manner of speaking."

"And I see you, probably every day."

"Or not."

"I see you and don't know it. That's part of the game you're playing."

"Let's say that it is. You like the idea I'm looking at you whether or not you know which observer I am. And you like to play this little power game on the phone. The one you're playing now."

"If I'm so terrible, why don't you call somebody else?"

"You know it's me calling. Why are you picking up?"

Silence.

Still silent.

"You can tell me anything," I said when she didn't hang up. "You can open your most secret self to me. Fearlessly."

There was another short silence. "You do get a little weird now and then."

I grinned. It wasn't like she was meeting me in a dark alley or anything, but she showed a kind of courage I liked. I was her obscene caller, and she had some mouth on her.

She added, "I can quit picking up the phone anytime."

"You won't do that. You like foreplay." "Foreplay" is a word I would never have used face to face with Patsy.

"I pick up because we're not faking it with each other," she said. "I don't have to be perfect for you. If I'm screwed up it's okay, because we both are. I don't have that with anyone else."

"That's your definition of being real? That you don't have to be perfect?" Who was she kidding? I get the imperfect Patsy and Biff gets the girl. I couldn't help laughing—a harsh noise, really.

"Laughter is like a fingerprint," she said. "I could recognize you from your laughter."

"If we were ever in a room together and I laughed," I said. "I'm not worried."

"I checked with the operator last night. This is a local call."

"It took you long enough to think of that," I said. My voice was steady, but my heart skipped a beat.

"I've been giving you a lot of thought," she said. "I know quite a bit about you."

I didn't like the turn this call had taken. "For openers?"

"Oh, don't try to sound so tough," she said with a delicate sneer in her voice. "You're much nicer than you want me to think."

"Just your local neighborhood pervert."

She answered, "You apologized for that, remember? You never say anything really devastating, even when you're being nasty."

"It's nice to hear you think so," I said on a sudden surge of emotion, but it didn't come out sounding all that nice. "You're not as self-centered as I thought, either."

She didn't react. At least, she didn't hang up.

"That's why you're doing this, isn't it? To get to know me."

I wanted to answer that with a resounding "maybe," but nothing came out. Originally I'd wanted to ask her out, but now she talked as if nothing was going on in her life but these calls. And I knew different.

She said, "It's hard for me to accept that I can be so terrifying, you have to resort to this. I don't have pointy teeth or long fingernails—"

"You think I'm scared of you? Is this your latest theory? Let me tell you, you do not lack for amazing ideas—" Okay, so I was getting a little out of hand.

"You trust me more than you know."

"How do you figure that?"

"I told you I spoke to the operator and you didn't hang up," she said, all blithe spirit. "You trusted me not to have this call traced."

She hung up. Quietly.

I had the feeling I'd lost this round.

I wasn't sure I trusted her, either.

Melanie and I had been at the bus stop for about five minutes. We said hi, and then nothing. Brown Bunny and Patsy came from opposite ends of the street at the same time. Patsy didn't appear to have lost any sleep over my phone call.

"So how was dinner with the uncle?" Melanie asked when Patsy got to the bus stop. "What's his mom like? And his dad?"

"His parents weren't there."

She and her friends talked about the most personal stuff in a normal voice. This made sense in New York City, where everyone was used to talking over the sound of traffic, but these neighborhoods were quiet. Everyone standing within twenty feet of these girls knew their business. Although Brown Bunny could not have looked less interested.

"Sort of boring," Patsy said. "He asked all the standard questions—what classes do I like, what are my plans for college, that kind of thing."

"Cool."

"No, just boring. He wanted to know if I mainly dated guys who were on a team. That bothered me, if you want to know the truth, and I got a little rude."

Brown Bunny came to life. "What did you say?"

"I said I had just started dating, I hadn't had time to become a groupie." This got a laugh, but I could see Patsy hadn't really been looking for that. "His wife kind of took over from there and talked about movies. It really wasn't an occasion, just a meal. I helped with the dishes."

"Did you get the feeling you were being checked out?" This was Melanie. "Like, are you good enough for him?"

"I don't know. Maybe. Hey, I got a call on Sunday," Patsy said, clearly finished with the dinner conversation.

"What kind of call?"

"An obscene phone call."

"You're kidding."

Patsy's expression squelched any doubts Melanie might

have had concerning the seriousness of her statement. "I've gotten a few of them. They started after that party I went to in Bayside. It could be one of those boys." She didn't add any pertinent details, like *And we're having conversations*.

Brown Bunny said, "Obscene callers are cowardly. Probably impotent except when they're on the phone."

"Not so loud," Melanie said. "It could be someone we know."

"I doubt it," Patsy said.

She didn't feel absolutely certain I went to school with her? I mean, she kept hammering away at making me admit to it. But maybe she wasn't as sure of herself as she seemed.

Patsy said, "Here comes the bus," and Brown Bunny said, "Hey, you didn't say. Did he ask you out for a real date?"

"Saturday."

Brown Bunny sat down with a guy who was already on the bus. Melanie and Patsy each took possession of two seats, setting their books on the empty one. A girl got on the bus at the next stop, carrying a couple of posters with pink frills. Talk turned to the Valentine's Day dance.

I sat at the back of the bus. I didn't let what Brown Bunny had to say about obscene callers touch me. It had nothing to do with me. She would understand that if she got to know me any better.

Which didn't seem very likely.

# TWENTY-SEVEN

Mom called to say she was getting home late, so I made dinner.

Buttered pumpernickel bread, some kind of soft lettuce that I found in the crisper, canned sardines with red onion and lemon. More of the lettuce as a salad.

Beer for Mr. B, a Coke for me.

Mr. B came to the table with a kind of quiet mood on him. He made some approving sounds as he chewed and then asked me, "So what's your thinking on basketball? You're tall, agile. You like basketball?"

Putting me on the spot.

I was not especially interested in dropping balls into baskets, not that it seemed a good idea to be that blunt.

Track.

Dad had an idea there. Nonviolent, big plus. At least I only had to worry about what I was doing, instead of a whole team. Also, I'd have the rest of the winter to get fit for spring meets. Longer if I couldn't qualify until next year. "I'm thinking track sounds like a possibility," I said, hoping to ease past making an actual commitment again.

I remembered then that Mr. B didn't actually coach the swim or track teams. The dean did.

"Are you fast?"

Who knew? I angled away with a question of my own. "What would I have to do to sign up?"

Mr. B said, "Consider yourself signed up."

It was almost a relief to be calling Patsy. Vincenzo might fail with Patsy, but his would not be a public embarrassment. Like failing at track. I'd spent most of the evening picturing the various ways in which I could humiliate myself on the track team.

She answered, saying, "Guess what?"

"I don't dare."

"Carlito!" she warned.

"Just tell me. Don't keep me in suspense."

"I'm on the Valentine's Day dance committee. It's going to be a masked ball."

I sensed something in the air, the way wild animals smell a trap. "Little eye masks?"

"Whole costumes. Romantic ones. Literary figures or theater characters, that's what they used to do. The drama teacher said we could do movie couples because it's, like, modern times."

"I guess that's cool."

"You could ask me to dance. Anonymously, of course."

"I don't dance."

"Unless you really are afraid of me." Terse. All business now.

"Not exactly."

"Then what?" she wanted to know. She'd begun using this demanding tone. "Well?"

"Maybe I don't want to see disappointment on your face."

"You're very pessimistic tonight."

"That's one word for it." She was right. Since committing to track, my mood had been low. I was contemplating taking up skiing after all, in hopes of breaking a leg.

"You're assuming a lot of not very nice things about me," she said. "That I wouldn't like you because you're . . . because you need to work, or because you're not very popular—oh, I don't know, whatever you are that you think I don't like."

"That's a deep thought, Patsy."

She sighed. "I know that sounds, um—"

"Have you ever dated someone your crowd wouldn't approve of?"

"How can I know that you're a person I wouldn't date if I don't meet you?"

"Then you admit to discriminatory practices?"

"I won't deny I'd say no to some people, Caesaro. Everyone has someone they'd say no to."

She'd had plenty of chances to look interested in me and

she never had. "You'll have to take my word for it. I'm the one."

"I don't have to take your word for anything. You're an anonymous caller."

"I'm an obscene caller."

"Why do you keep talking through that handkerchief?"

"It's how this sort of thing is done."

"What sort of thing? We're talking, that's all."

"That's what you're doing."

Sharp intake of breath.

I waited a couple of beats. "What do you think obscene callers do wh—"

Click.

I hung up, my chest aching hollowly for—Patsy? I sighed. If this was love . . .

# TWENTY-EIGHT

The next morning, I made a simulated run.

My eventual goal would be to run all the way to school and then run around the track a few times. I'd have to work up to it over two or three days. But I wanted to get the feel for it, run partway—three, four blocks. Then jog back and take the bus like any other morning. By next week, I'd be ready to do the run and start to work on speed.

I set my clock for an hour earlier, for five-thirty. There is no way to simulate a five-thirty rising in winter. It's still dark at five-thirty, and it is *cold*.

It took me half an hour to do the warm-ups, but I reasoned that when I ran all the way to school, that would count toward the overall run.

Right from the start, my jeans kept making this sound like a nail file. Half a block on, the bottoms of my pants felt like they got caught on my ankles or wrapped around them. I had to walk part of the next block to catch my breath anyway. I started to run again, but this time I couldn't go as far before I had to walk. I was wheezing.

On the third block, I developed a stitch in my right side. It was a good thing I called this a simulated run. I turned around to go home, walking. I managed to avoid a face-to-face with Mr. B without actually hiding from him, which was a relief to me. I lay down for ten minutes, then took a hot shower and practiced breathing. It hurt.

Mr. B had gone by the time I got downstairs, and Mom was on her way out. She was dressed for the office, wearing those stubby running shoes. She carried her chunky heels in a shopping bag. "Headed for work?" I asked her in a chatty way.

"Of course. I'm still bringing in a paycheck," she said. "Even if I'm not the only one."

Something had wound up her clock. I didn't know what it was, and I didn't want to find out. We left together. Mom went one way, heading for the train. I went the other.

The day had a bright side. I got an A plus on my book report. Also, that was the last of the makeup homework having to do with changing schools in November.

At first it just felt like my mood was lighter. But I soon saw the girls were all atwitter, making plans for the dance.

That night I asked Mr. B about running clothes.

"For the time being, you won't need anything but a good pair of running shoes. Those sneakers you're wearing won't do. And we'll get you a sweat suit. I don't guess you've got one."

"No, I guess not," I said, to be agreeable.

"Vinnie, you have a sweat suit," Mom said irritably. She was right, but it was still in my closet, in a box I hadn't unpacked since the move. I'd forgotten about it.

Then, roused like a bear from hibernation, she turned on Mr. B. "Why wouldn't he have a sweat suit?"

Dad and I know enough never to answer Mom's questions when they follow an indication that her fur's been mussed. Mr. B didn't understand this yet.

"It's only that he's never been athletically inclined, Donna. I just assumed—"

"The way you're assuming he's 'never' been athletically inclined?"

"I'm talking about his interests—"

"Not all athletics revolve around football, Dominic." Ooh, Mom catches on fast.

"Just what athletics are you talking about, Donna?" Mr. B was sounding a little testy himself.

"He did okay in gymnastics last year, didn't he?"

In all fairness, that's how I did. Okay. And that good only when I hoped it would discourage further meetings between Mom and Mr. B. Not that it was a good time to point that out.

Mom wouldn't quit while she was ahead. "When he was eight years old, he could run back and forth along the seesaw to keep it level. You know, keeping it moving without letting it touch the ground," Mom said, finishing on an uncertain note. "That was athletic."

Mom was right. That's why I fell and broke my nose at the tender age of eight.

"And he can dance," she added.

Mr. B sized up the situation and set his face to a carefully neutral expression. He told my mother what she wanted to hear. "Vinnie and I haven't talked much about his interests, Donna. I'm happy he's going out for track, really I am." Mr. B seemed to have developed a British accent.

"Did you hear that, Vinnie?"

She didn't want much from him. Just total capitulation.

"Sure, Mom." Chalk one up on the down side for the stepdad.

Patsy said, "You weren't so nice to me last night, Dominic."

"No, I wasn't." Actually, she gave me something of a turn, coming up with Mr. B's name. I drew in a slow, deep breath.

"I'm not sure I like you when you get into that mood."

"I didn't know you liked me at all."

"What a strange thing to say." She tapped the receiver while she thought it over, a rapid heartbeat. I slid deeper into my bed, embarrassed somehow. Excruciatingly embarrassed.

"I've been thinking, you must really need to talk to someone. Anonymously, you know? Otherwise, why the handkerchief?"

"What's with you and the handkerchief? You need one?"

"You're pretty funny, Domino."

"Go ahead! Make fun. Every time you waste the chance to guess my name, the likelier it is we'll have to go around again."

"Sounds like you're counting on a lot of calls."

There was a soft click. At first I wasn't sure she'd hung up. "Patsy?" Nothing. Then the dial tone.

Go figure.


The next morning I unpacked the running suit my mom was talking about. Bright blue in a fabric as slippery as gym shorts. I wouldn't be keeping a low profile. I'd run a little, then walk to school. Maybe sprint two or three times.

At the back door, I met the next obstacle to my running career. Something that had not occurred to me during my simulated run. How was I going to carry my books? I could hardly run while holding them against my chest. I left them, along with my folded jeans, in Mr. B's place at the table, he'd bring them to school this time.

It was about a twelve-block run to the school. Just about a mile, Mr. B told me. It was cold out, but he'd also said I'd warm up quick. Strangely enough, the first block wasn't bad.

If only I hadn't talked myself into running longer. By the time I made five blocks, I was finished. I turned around and walked back home. My head ached. I had worked up just enough of a sweat to feel a chill coming on. It made a person think. If modern man can't run five blocks, how's he going to make it as far as the next millennium?

About halfway home, I decided to run the last block so I wouldn't look like such a loser. As I gathered strength for the burst of energy needed to run that last block, I thought, I'll have to get up earlier in the morning. Much earlier.

Mom and Mr. B were just finishing breakfast as I got back. Which meant she was having coffee. And he was having coffee and Ritz crackers with strawberry jelly. Yum.

"So. How was it?" Mr. B wanted to know. He poured himself another cup of coffee. No doubt he had made the coffee if he wanted seconds.

"Good," I said, trying not to sound like I was choking to death. Hard to do when my throat was clogged with ropy saliva. I reached for the orange juice and drank straight from the carton.

"Vinnie," Mom complained as she folded a sheet of newspaper. An auspicious horoscope, no doubt.

"It's hard in the beginning," Mr. B said. He knew how it was going, how it was really going.

I didn't volunteer anything but to share my scrambled eggs. Mr. B hovered around the stove while I stirred the eggs with shaking hands. He rescued the toast in the nick of time and sat down for a second meal.

# TWENTY-NINE

Because I got to the stop just as the bus driver was about to pull away, I managed to avoid the usual awkward pretense of hardly noticing Patsy. It was almost natural that I didn't look at her, even as I claimed the seat directly behind her. However, I overheard part of a conversation with Melanie.

"There must be a thousand names for boys!" she said.

"I don't know what they are, Patsy. What class do you need them for, anyway?"

"The new gym teacher is Italian, right?" She turned around suddenly and speared me with a look. "What's your name?"

"My name is Gold. Jewish." I said it without thinking. Without realizing it, I had sidestepped her real question with a technicality. "Dom's my stepfather."

Melanie looked shocked. "Patsy!"

"I'm sorry. I didn't mean to be rude," she said, and turned back.

Melanie said, "I can't believe the way you act sometimes."

"Me either."


I called Dad and told him, "I'm going out for track."

"Good. I think. No one swinging a lethal weapon, no one behaving like a lethal weapon?"

"It's cool."

"I was on the track team for about twenty minutes," Dad said, and went on to tell me a few stories. Locker room pranks and smelling of Ben-Gay instead of aftershave on dates played a big part in his reminiscences. He seemed to have happy memories about that time even though a broken heel polished off his brief running career. He mentioned he'd worn a backpack to school.

"Oh, right, I've been wondering what to do with my books." I'd seen a few guys using backpacks, but I carried my books propped against my hip. Now I wondered if those guys were the track team.

"Mona's here, she wants to say hi," Dad said as we signed off.

"I don't know what you said," she whispered. "But he hasn't laughed like that in weeks. You made him feel good."

"Me too," I said, realizing it was true.

* * *

"You aren't *extremely* short, are you, Eduardo?" She didn't sound bored or playful, she was on the attack.

"Why?"

"Some guys worry about being shorter than girls."

"Some *girls* worry about that." But it was an interesting question. "Are we deciding whether I'm datable?"

"No. All right, yes," she said. "But not necessarily for me."

"You have another number you want me to call?"

"No, I— Oh, all right, I was asking for me."

"I haven't asked you out."

"I don't need to wait for you to do the asking, Eggo."

"So are you?" I was suddenly tense. This was about the dance.

"Asking?" she wanted to know.

"Uh-huh."

"No."

I breathed a sigh of relief. "Not enough data?"

"It's not that I'd ask or say yes if *you* asked. I don't go out with perverts. I'm just curious about you, I guess."

"That kind of thing is highly detrimental to relationships."

"What kind of thing?"

"When you don't have a comeback, you dredge up old stuff to say."

"Your 'old stuff' is a felony," she said.

"Misdemeanor. Six months' probation."

"You sound awfully sure about that. Been checking into it, just in case?"

I said, "You may not even be my type."

"What type is that?"

"Nice."

"Yeah, I can see how that'd be a problem."

"See what I mean?"

"How come you always call at twelve o'clock?"

"I'm a traditional kind of guy."

"You could call later some nights."

I had a feeling I knew where she was going with this, but I asked anyway. "When, for instance?"

"Saturday night?" Very coy.

I checked in with what Vinnie knew and Vincenzo shouldn't. "Maybe you're going out?"

"What if I'm not here at midnight?"

"I won't call again."

"Ever?"

I lay in the darkness of my room, strong and silent.

"That's stupid," she said, her voice full of outrage.

I didn't respond. But she was right. It was stupid.

"Ooh, the strong, silent type." Contempt.

"I'm taking notes," I said, and like I really was, I spaced out my next words. "Gets . . . mean . . . when . . . frustrated . . . Name-calling."

"You're trying to make me hang up," she said.

"So? Are you going to fall for that?"

"No. I'm just going to say good night."

Click.

I had a strong mental image of her, lips parted over small white teeth. Sitting with her finger pressed viciously on the button, springing the trap. I turned on my reading lamp. Vincenzo was at his best in the dark, but I had to see more clearly.

Was she telling me she'd go out with me if I asked? Was she serious? Or was this a trick to bring me out into the light?

I switched off my lamp.

I started out on Thursday morning with confidence, running with graceful strides punctuated by the shifting weight of a backpack supplied by Mr. B. It helped. My arms were free; I felt balanced.

I took an alternate route that would bypass the bus stop and the pointed once- and twice-over Patsy was giving everyone these days. I was well into the next block before I dropped back to a walk to catch my breath.

My throat was on fire, each gasp fanned the flames. I had to walk longer between each bout of running. "Bout" is an appropriate word. I was fighting all the way. The one good thing I could think of, since I'd gone this way, nobody who mattered could see how close to failure I was.

I walked the rest of the way to school.

There were members of various teams jogging around the track and several health-oriented taxpayers pacing themselves as they followed the runners around and around. I went straight indoors and headed for the library, where I waited for the first bell.

In homeroom, I was given a note to see the guidance counselor, a beefy guy with a red face, he looked permanently sunburned. He greeted me with one word: "Gold!"

I'd met him once before, when classes were assigned. It seemed he always talked like he'd just come across someone he'd known for years.

"Got a schedule change for ya!"

"Excuse me?"

"We're bumping you up in English, and in order to do that, we had to shift your science and gym classes."

"Why?"

"Your English teacher says you're bored! You write well! You need an A-level class. That will be Mrs. Saunders, room 203. Start today, first period! All your teachers have been informed."

So first period I parked myself three desks behind Patsy's.

And in third period, I learned I'd been put in Biff's gym class.

I didn't take the bus home, but tried again. Run, walk, run, walk. The backpack worked out, that was the only thing that did. I could've talked to Mr. B, but I wanted him to see me as a guy who was toughing it out. So I called Dad again, hoping he'd have some practical advice for the beginning runner.

I dialed. We talked for about two minutes, just enough time for me to brag a little about being bumped up in English, before Dad said, "Hey, Vinnie, can we talk tomorrow?"

"Working?" The man was going to make a million.

"I don't want to be late."

"Okay." But driving the taxi didn't mean punching a clock by a certain time. Dad showed up at the garage and waited for someone to drive in because it was the end of their day. Then he gassed up and drove out.

Unless somebody was making a movie. Then he made sure he'd have a car by a certain time. I wasn't trying to hold him up, but I asked, "The taxi's got a job?"

"I've got a date, Vinnie."

I felt like a sprinkle of cold water hit me. "I didn't know."

"I should've told you."

Right. At least mentioned that he was interested in somebody. That he was going to ask her out. We talked to each other just about every other day.

I guess we all have our little secrets.

I said, "So listen, we'll talk tomorrow."

"It's just that I'm running late."

"Go. Tomorrow," I said, and hung up. I felt kind of bad because I was somebody he couldn't confide in.

Of course, I wasn't exactly confiding in him either. What

could I say? *Hey, Dad, it's a few calls, that's all, no harm done. Nobody's going to know it's me, plenty of people have Patsy's phone number. Biff has her phone number.*

If I'd opened a window, a cold draft would have blown in. It couldn't have been any colder than the realization I had right then that Biff was probably calling her every night too.

# THIRTY

"Frederico?"

"You were expecting another caller?"

"Was I a snot last night? I didn't mean to be."

"That's all right. Short guys are used to being the butt of jokes."

"It's okay then?" she asked. "You'll call later on Saturday nights."

"Oh, so now it's more than one. Cheating on me, are you?"

"We're not dating," she said.

And so, hardly exclusive. "No, we aren't."

"You sound a little down," she said, and hesitated. "Usually you snap back at me like a rubber band."

"Everything's fine" was all I managed.

"Come on," she said. I suppose I could say she was wheedling, but it sounded much more attractive than that. Like real concern. "Girl trouble?"

"Not my girl." Froglike. My voice didn't sound like my own.

"Whose?"

"My dad got himself one." I felt better just saying it out loud. And it seemed to me that she might be more forthcoming about Biff if I set the tone with a confidence of my own.

"A girl?"

"I suppose she's older than that. I could see he would, eventually. It's just that he didn't tell me about her. I'm feeling a little left out, I guess."

"You see a lot of him?"

"I used to."

"You'll still get to."

"Oh, yeah," I said, shrugging in the darkness. Self-pitying, okay, but it felt good for just that minute.

"He'll be happier if this works out. You want him to be happy, right?"

"I guess I'm being childish."

"You are his child."

"Good point." Suddenly I felt like grinning. The funny thing, she helped. I didn't feel such a pressure to "handle" this thing with my dad. I mean, what was I supposed to do? Nothing, that's what.

She was quiet for a minute, and I just listened to her breathe.

It was pretty nice, actually. That we could just be there, breathing, and not saying anything.

"I'm sorry I give you such a hard time," she said.

"Are you serious? I've got a two-minute window before your next wisecrack."

"You don't think I'm really sorry?"

"Have you spoken to anyone about this neurotic need to apologize?"

"Please don't do that," she said, and her tone of voice threw me. Not asking, not ordering, but communicating a real need to talk to me. To hear what I had to say. But I guess she'd done that before. Maybe it was the first time we were both ready at the same time. Maybe that was it.

"Maybe we ought to hang up now," I said. "Before we ruin what seems to be a good moment."

"Or you could tell me about the valentine you're going to give me." Her flirty voice.

Of course. I could give her a card and know that she'd be eager to find it. Why hadn't I thought of it? And why was I suddenly feeling reluctant? Well, for one thing, it called for a disclosure.

"I guess I could slip it into your locker," I said.

"So you're giving me one?"

"Are you setting up cameras?"

"Francesco." Sort of dragging it out. Wheedling.

"I'm trying to figure out how I'd sign it. 'Anonymous Admirer' doesn't quite do it."

"I've been thinking about us, Fabio," she said. "You call back, wanting to know what I'll say, we argue, get mad."

I drew back, not just away from the receiver, but my whole insides cringed. "I'm listening."

"You care. And still, we only talk on the phone."

"Yeah?"

"I thought you were embarrassed to be found out," she said. "That I'd tell someone what you'd done. I don't think that anymore."

"Just when I was starting to feel so good about us." She was getting on my nerves.

"I think you don't let anyone get close. You're afraid someone *will* love you."

"A lot depends upon which someone we're talking about."

She said, "Let me ask you something. My pick, like playing Twenty Questions."

"I have to answer?"

"How else am I supposed to guess who you are?" she said.

"I don't think we're playing the same game." It was all slippery muck I was standing on, but I was finding my footing. When she made an exasperated sound, I added, "A one-time question or a to-be-continued, like my name?"

"One time only," she conceded.

"Okay."

"You'll be honest?"

"One time only."

"Have we ever spoken to each other?" she asked. "Off the phone, I mean. Are you somebody I talk to every day but don't notice, like somebody who shelves books in the library or sits at a desk near mine?"

I laughed out loud, a real laugh. I don't know why exactly. I was perspiring all of a sudden. "That's all you want to ask?"

"What would you suggest?"

"If I could ask you any question, I could come up with something better than that."

"Just answer, Fandango," she said in an annoyed tone.

"No," I answered, chuckling reassuringly. "We don't talk. No shared classes."

That's right. I lied. What would you have done?

A breathy, impatient sound traveled over the line. I imagined feeling the puff of air in my ear. "So can I?" I asked her.

"Can you what?"

"Ask you anything I want to."

Click.

Guess not.


I got up late for running, but the sun was shining—that was the upside. I decided to skip breakfast, do the alternating thing of walk some, run some. Ten minutes later, the sun was not shining.

It was a cold, crummy morning, and as I jogged past the as-yet-unpopulated bus stop, a drizzly rain started to fall, adding to the misery of being outside in the cold when half an hour before I'd been in a warm bed. That was the down-side.

My head ached in the cold, but I got into a stride. The walk-run stride. It wasn't poetry. I'd nearly reached the school when my unfed energy began to flag, seriously flag.

Blood was pounding so loudly in my ears that I didn't hear the school bus coming, and it passed me just as I gave up and bent over at the waist, gagging. I was too miserable to take note of how much of an audience I had, or who was part of it.

Oh, and here's the best part. Changing up to an A class? More homework to make up. Three essays and a test.

In class, Patsy turned around and offered up a sympathetic pout. I sent back a devil-may-care grin, but she'd turned back too quickly to catch it.

I decided to take a turn around the track after school.

That was when I saw Patsy on the bleachers, looking cold but determined. I tried to tell myself she was waiting for the late bus. But that bus came and went with the other girls who'd been milling around the gym, talking decorations. Patsy stretched her jacket over her knees for warmth and watched the guys speeding around the track.

I hated knowing she could also watch me.

I ran faster and not especially well, thinking about how I looked. I tightened up, didn't get enough air. I was out of breath sooner than I should have been. The wind was picking up and made my eyes water. Pretty soon my nose was running. I cramped up.

I got off the track and into the locker room. It was a terrible run.

Dad called that evening. I waited for him to say something about the date, where our last conversation broke off, and tell me where he met her or something. But he went straight to "How's the running going?"

"Better every day," I lied. "I'm turning out to be the athletic type after all."

"Great," Dad said.

"Yeah," I said. "Tomorrow morning I expect to make it to the end of the block."

Dad laughed, first in surprise and then gratefully, knowing how hard it was for me to admit to the possibility of failure. We never did get around to talking about his date, but I was in no mood to hold that against him.

# THIRTY-ONE

I wondered if I was wrong to lie to Patsy, and then I wondered if it mattered. Vinnie was never going to get a shot at dating her anyway.

"Giorgio."

"You sound soggy."

"How can one word sound soggy?"

"I'm not a total jerk. I can tell you've been crying."

"Some people would pretend they didn't notice."

"Some people would," I agreed. "So why are you crying?"

"That's none of your business," she said, after a long moment. "It's none of my business, even." And while I was wondering what that meant, she made a little kitten sound, crying. She asked, "What do you think about married people having sex?"

I tried not to think about that. "I believe they generally do."

"I can't talk to anybody else about this," she said, the tension cracking her voice. Total surrender.

Fear curled deep in my belly. "Are they having it with each other?"

She giggled and stopped, then laughed in a hiccuppy way.

I said, "I know that sounded stupid."

"Somebody else," she said, still giggling. I had a feeling there were tears as well. "They're having it with someone else."

"As in swapping?"

"No. As in one person having an affair. I shouldn't—"

"It's out now. Keep talking."

"I'm talking too much. It's one of my parents. The other one knows, but—I don't want to talk about them."

"You want to just sit here in the dark and be quiet?"

"Are you sitting in the dark?"

I lost only a split second before I said, as if amazed, "You mean you aren't?"

"I just never thought of it," she said.

"Oh, *now* I don't feel you've been taking these calls seriously enough."

"Seriously enough for what?"

"I feel so used."

She laughed. "Cut that out."

"Here I believed you loved me the way I love you, as a dark and secret thing."

"You love me?"

"Only as a dark and secret thing."

"Just so we understand each other," she said, and hung up.

I had a warm and happy glow going as I put the phone down. I had the feeling we did understand each other. Sort of.

Mom shook me awake on Saturday. "Vinnie, it's past noon."

"It's the weekend, Mom." I didn't have to get up while it was still dark out. I didn't have to run until I threw up my meager breakfast. "The. Week. End."

"Get up now or you'll never get to sleep tonight, you'll want to get up even later tomorrow morning, and by Monday you'll just be getting to sleep when you ought to be getting up."

This is a mother's logic, and I'd heard it before. I rolled out, landing flat on the floor. She jabbed me in the ribs with a toe. "Up."

She was in one of her businessy moods. Feeling very efficient. All I can say is, when she's home for the day, this is wasted energy. Everybody's wasted energy.

She spent a lot of time making lists and scribbling on index cards. This morning, she tacked up a chart in the dining room. It didn't reflect schedules so much as the division of labor. I noticed most of the labor fell to Mr. B and me, while Mom covered us in the shopping and carrying-dry-cleaning department. Neither Mr. B nor I have much dry cleaning to worry about.

Mom hadn't finished making entries on the chart, she was still shifting index cards around on the table, each card representing a task to be carried out. I looked over her shoulder and saw that the row of cards she consistently left in place were marked "Dinner Mon," "Dinner Tues," "Dinner Wed," and so on.

"Vinnie, weren't you getting home from school earlier last week?"

"I'm running now, Mom."

"Yes, but that doesn't take all that long, does it? You like to cook a whole lot more than you like running. I'm thinking you could start dinner when you get home."

There was a catch in my breathing all of a sudden, and it had nothing to do with running. "You mean pop a casserole in the oven or something?"

"I mean, I'll tell you what's for dinner, and you could start chopping onions and cleaning the chicken or whatever."

"Something like what Dad used to do, you mean?"

"Exactly. You like to cook, Vinnie."

I was seized with a dark and not unreasonable anger. It lodged in my throat, making my words come out choked and oddly spaced. "I think it's time you learned how to get along in the kitchen on your own, Mom."

My mother's features slipped and blurred, shifting again to a trembling fury. "What did you say?"

"You had that arrangement with Dad and you gave it up. You have a new setup with Mr. B. I'm not responsible for anything you overlooked!" I was shouting everything. I don't know how I got so angry so quickly. "You want a cook, you make enough money to hire one."

"Get out!" she yelled. "Out!"

It shook me, but I stood my ground. "Out? You want me to move out?"

"No," she gasped. "No, I . . . I meant, go to your room. I want you out of my sight!"

I let my manner imply that I knew better but I was letting it pass. But my hands were shaking. I could hear my mother crying until I closed my bedroom door. I felt like I had a wooden stake buried in my heart. If I could just reach in and tear the whole mess out, I'd be better off.

I didn't feel any better an hour later when Mr. B came upstairs to tell me he had decided to take my mother out for lunch. A message delivered in somber tones. This was no doubt inspired by my mother's emotional upset. She probably felt as bad as I did, maybe worse. But my sympathy went to Mr. B. The bachelor life must have begun to seem like one of his fondest memories.

# THIRTY-TWO

Dad dropped by later in the day. He came to the door, knocked, and, when I answered it, asked if I wanted to go for a ride. I got my jacket, wondering if Mom had called him.

"Did Mom call you today?" I asked as I got into the front seat.

"No, why?"

"No reason."

"I got a fare for a wedding out here today. I have to go pick them up later, get them back to the airport in time for a flight. So we can hang out for a couple of hours."

Because it was so sunny and looked like it *ought* to be warm, we drove with the windows down, letting the air blast us. We got cold, but we did it anyway for about half an hour. Then we rolled up the windows without saying why.

I knew Dad had something he wanted to tell me. Man to

man. In the spirit of shared confidences, I told Dad about the leather pants. It felt like such a long time ago, it seemed almost funny to me now. I made it funny, anyway. Dad laughed so hard he had to pull over and wipe the tears from his eyes.

But when I said, "Anything new in your life?" Dad answered, "Not much."

"Nothing at all?"

"Nothing to talk about just yet." We looked at each other and looked away. Dad rescued the moment, asking, "You got the tank set up yet?"

"There's a lot to read up on."

"Give me a call if you run into a problem."

"Sure, Dad."

I felt like an awkwardness stayed with us for the next hour. We got the hang of saying something into those spaces where it was most obvious, and it got better. But not necessarily comfortable. Like swimming.

Mr. B's car was in the driveway when Dad dropped me back home. Things were back to normal, if a little quieter than usual. I could hear Mom talking about taking a painting class, Mr. B making encouraging noises. I stood at the kitchen window, and I was there when the Lincoln hummed into the driveway.

Biff got out, dressed like a guy on a date for once, not like he was about to knock heads in a scrimmage. No doubt he had a big night planned. I turned away and went to say hello to Mom and Mr. B.

Would Patsy come home in time? Or did I mean so little to her that she could toss our conversations aside? I could call her again tonight.

Of course, I'd no longer have the upper hand.

Then again, did I ever? She was out on a date, and I was waiting for her to come home.

Dinner was spaghetti and meatballs from the deli section of the supermarket. The crepe paper–green parsley flakes they used for garnish were a dead giveaway. However, Mr. B didn't complain, and I didn't either.

I went upstairs to write a book report, thinking about everything but. I wrote badly. By ten o'clock, I was haunting the windows, hoping to see Patsy come home.

At 11:35, the car pulled up in front of her house.

I'd been sitting near the window, and I heard the car idling. I could look out from behind the edge of my curtains without getting up from my desk.

They sat there till 11:53. If she'd known I could see her, or at least the car she sat in, I'd have accused Patsy of playing with me. Finally, she burst out of the car. That's how it looked. She ran up the sidewalk. Biff got out and followed her partway, then stopped and sort of wandered back to his car. Odd.

I didn't have time to think about it. It was twelve a.m. I dialed. I reached to switch off my lamp, then caught myself. If she sat anywhere near a window while she waited for the phone to ring, she might notice that my light always went out just before the first ring. I left it alone.

Ringing.

"Ignatio?" From underwater. Like a clogged drain. "I couldn't find an H name."

"There aren't many," I said, adrenaline coursing through my veins. I was still worried about the lamp. It's just this kind of little detail that trips up big criminals.

"I thought you were going to call later tonight."

"Don't pick a fight, okay? What's wrong? You don't sound too good."

"Maybe you should've called someone else," she answered back. She was quick, but she didn't have the usual snap.

"I called you."

She said, "Nasty habit."

"They say that makes the best . . . partnerships. Whatever." It felt strange, talking to her with the light on. Personal. Like asking her into my room.

"What does?"

"One person's neurosis neatly fitted into someone else's."

I figured she'd object to the idea she might have a neurosis, but she said, "I went out tonight. He wouldn't let me out of the car."

"What?"

"He tried to make like he was joking. I told him I didn't want to mess around, but he wouldn't give it up."

"What did you do?" I got up and started to pace, three

steps away and three steps back, pulling the phone cord with me. All this crap going on while I'm watching from the window and I can't even tell.

"I grabbed the ashtray and dumped it in his lap. Some of the ashes were still hot. He thinks smoking looks smart. Anyway, I jumped out while he was yelling and brushing himself off."

"Why'd you go out with him?" I was angry and I didn't try to hide it. Anything was better than the slipping, sliding dread that made me weak. "I mean, couldn't you tell Biff was a jerk?"

"All my friends think he's pretty cool."

"They've been out with him, these girls?"

"He's a big shot in school. You know how it is, Iggy. My friends see me as something like the leader of our group. So they thought it was cool that he asked me out."

"Clique," I said, feeling another queasy ripple of adrenaline in my veins.

"What?"

"That's what your group is. A clique. Like you're too good for most and very choosy about the rest."

"That's your opinion," she said shakily.

"And you know what else?" I yelled.

"What?"

"If you're the leader, how come you're doing what they tell you—"

Click.

Then again, maybe those friends didn't have as much of an influence as she claimed. She sure didn't care what I thought.

On Sunday, Mom and Mr. B had a day planned. Mr. B was keeping us in separate corners till the room cooled, the way he did with guys who got hot under the collar in gym class. He said he'd drive into the city with her, walk around a little, see a matinee, go out to dinner.

Mom poked her nose into my room to give me a run-down on the sandwich supplies. I could've gone out for a so-called run while they got ready. Instead, I holed up in my room, muttering to myself over the poorly written instruction sheet for the fish tank's air pump.

Mr. B brought me a fried egg sandwich as if he was accustomed to cheerfully bringing obnoxious people breakfast in bed. He was in and out quickly so he could dress for the day, and I could hear Mom using that chirpy little voice she'd reserved for him when they were dating.

My mood started to improve. That odd little chirp in Mom's voice had bothered me a few months ago, but not anymore. I'd realized it was the voice of my mom being happy. I wanted her to be happy. And I wanted him to be happy. I didn't think of Mr. B as a dad, but I thought of him as family.

After they'd gone, I set to work on the fish tank. For about three hours I muddled through, washing gravel, playing nice with a plastic Oriental bridge with attached bonsai-like trees, sorting out the filtering system.

When I added water and got it all working, I spent an hour getting my homework finished. By then it was late enough that Mom and Mr. B would be headed for the restaurant. And I was hungry.

# THIRTY-THREE

I looked in the fridge to see what my options were. Another egg sandwich or PB&J. And of course there were the deli packages, paper-wrapped.

But I found a few small zucchini in the same crisper. Mom only bought vegetables that were out of season. Her urge to enjoy them lasted until she was faced with the problem of how to cook them.

The zucchini made me want to sit down to Dad's cooking. I went through the contents of the kitchen shelves and found a box of linguini. Uh-huh, I said to myself as I chose a small can of chopped tomatoes, another of mushrooms. Back to the fridge. A rather soft onion. Cream, for Mr. B's coffee, but I wouldn't use it all. Good enough.

I'd make a variation on a pasta-and-sour-cream dish

Dad used to make the night before he had a busy day of auditions. Whoever got in first put it into the oven to reheat. But I could make the sauce while the pot boiled and have a hot meal in half an hour.

Once I'd collected the main ingredients, I turned on the radio, unbuttoned a couple of shirt buttons, and flipped up my collar. Vincenzo was cooking tonight.

I was giving the spaghetti a toss when someone knocked at the kitchen door. Snatching at a sauced stick of zucchini, I popped it into my mouth as I answered the door. Patsy was standing outside, shivering in a soft dark sweater with a wide neck that left one shoulder to fend for itself in the cold.

"Hi. I thought since we're neighbors . . . ," she said, and shivered. "Can I come in?"

"Sure." God. Maybe she'd guessed. Guessed but wasn't sure.

Her eyes slid past me to the spaghetti dish. And then, as if she might bolt, she added, "Didn't your parents go out?"

"They did," I said, licking my fingers free of the sauce. She'd been watching? I stepped back so she could come in. Might as well learn the worst.

"I have a kind of favor to ask and I hope you won't be offended." All at once she sounded less sure of herself than the Patsy I knew, and she looked decidedly uncomfortable. "See, I need some Italian first names. Men's names, and your stepdad is Italian."

This visit wasn't about me. At least it wasn't about making an accusation. I hoped it was okay to be talking to her like this—my T-shirt was being put to the test.

"Italian first names?" she repeated, like maybe I hadn't been paying attention.

I decided not to catch on too quick. "What are they?"

She said, "I don't know."

I turned obtuse up to maximum. "I gathered you don't know, but if you don't give him the list, how can he translate?"

"I don't need a translation. I want him to *give* me a list. Just go through the alphabet and give me a few names for each letter. Do you think he would do that?"

I said, "I guess so," but what I wanted to say, the way she said it to me, she must be counting on a lot of calls. "You know"—I walked over to the fridge—"the Italian alphabet doesn't have as many letters as we do."

"What do you mean?"

"The *H* is silent, so it's . . ." I reached into the fridge for a bottle of wine. Taboo, but I was showing off. Patsy didn't comment, but her eyes were wide open when I looked at her over my shoulder. "Um, Henry becomes Enrico." I rolled the *r* and put the swing in the "rico."

"Really."

I hesitated to offer further illumination. After all, how much should I know? And I thought Vinnie ought to be a little less, well, verbal than Vincenzo. But willing to talk, because who wouldn't be?

"How do you know that?" I saw a flash of hunger in her eyes.

"I asked when I heard it. I'm curious."

"So," she said. "*J?*"

I shook my head. "An Italian name would start with a G." I'd hit a pedantic note, and it was just right. Italian-name nerd.

"Are any other letters missing?" she asked.

"*K, W, X,* and *Y.*"

"*W?* I never noticed."

"Elmer Fudd probably didn't have an Italian heritage." I grinned. "You know, 'wascally wabbit'?"

She laughed. We were having a nice little conversation here. Which was what I wanted, after all. But now I was afraid she'd somehow leap to asking what names start with V, the way people in the same room sometimes come up with the same thought. I knew this was crazy, but I started to want her to leave.

"Thanks." She turned on her brilliant response-to-applause smile, the kind of smile she used for peons who only wanted to pick up her books when she dropped them. I didn't like feeling like a peon. I winked in a friendly way, hoping to set us back on even ground. But her smile faltered, then flattened to a phony paste-on as she let herself out. "Bye, Vinnie."

I took a deep breath, letting the tension go.

I tried to sort through the ups and downs of this episode. I hadn't offered her much of myself at all. Except for a moment there that I could be proud of, I was doing a bit, like

Dad sometimes pulls out of the air. It could have been a limp, a stutter, anything. This was a superior, holier-than-thou attitude that outdid Patsy's own natural self-love.

In fact, I didn't know why I wanted to do that. I had finally made contact, real face-to-face contact with her, and did I try to put in a good word for myself?

No.

I crossed the kitchen in two steps and yanked the door open. She was just standing in the driveway, arms crossed against the cold. Her house was dark except for the front light. "Hey," I called. "You hungry?"

She turned and came back fast, saying, "Cold and hungry. Are you feeding strays?"

I didn't have a comeback. I just grinned and shut the door behind her.

"You cooked this?" She sidled up to the table and looked at it from a funny angle, sort of down her nose. She was nervous—I got that—but she was hungry, too.

"Sautéed matchsticks of zucchini and linguini blanketed in a creamy tomato sauce," I said in a rough impersonation of Julia Child.

"What's creamy tomato sauce?"

"Southern Italian specialty."

"Your dad taught you?"

"Just so we're clear, Mr. B is not my dad." She watched as I poured two inches of wine into glasses.

"Mr. B, then. Who taught you how to cook an Italian dish?" Patsy asked a tad too casually.

"You think they're keeping it a national secret? We all like good food. Plates in the cabinet behind you. So what do you need these names for?"

"Oh, it's a long story," she said, setting the plates on the table. "Too long. Boring."

I started loading on the spaghetti. I let her lack of explanation hang between us. Her face grew rosy.

I sat. And I let her off the hook. "You going to eat or you going to let it get cold?"

Dinner was easy. We started to talk about the class we shared.

And we decided to watch a movie after we did the dishes. *Love Story* was on TV. For a minute I let myself bask in the warmth of life's little gifts—a good movie and I'm alone with Patsy.

I spent some time wondering whether it would be construed as a pass if I just let my arm fall along the back of the sofa. I wondered if she'd freak out after last night's date with Biff. I doubted it; she wasn't sitting all that close anyway. But she didn't know that's the way I sit most of the time. It really is.

We'd just about gotten to the really sad part when Patsy complained about her foot. Loudly.

"What is it?"

"Asleep. It's gone to sleep," she moaned, lifting it off the floor. The movement seemed to be painful.

"Shake it. Rub it."

"No," she yelled. "Don't touch it."

Too late. I pulled off her sneaker, which was the first shock, feeling her shoe so small in my hand. It should have prepared me for the warmth of her foot. But it didn't. It didn't. I understood in a flash all that I was meant to know the night of the junior dance. I told myself that was a silly notion. I gave her foot a hard rub, trying to dispel the sense of falling backward, of falling under a spell.

"Ow, ow, ow," Patsy was yelling.

"You have to get the blood to circulate. Let's get it moving," I said unsympathetically, and gave it another vigorous rub.

"Ow, stop. It'll get better on its own."

I slid into the space beside her as she turned to put her foot on the floor. I had just a glimpse of the surprise on her face as I used my knee to adjust her position to suit mine and settled back into the film. Or appeared to.

What I was doing, while my heart was beating a mile a minute, was thinking about how easy it had been to get an arm behind her, to be practically wrapped around her although we weren't actually touching anywhere now, and, after all the agony, how comfortable it was to be sitting that way. No sweaty palms, no awkward glances to check whether it was okay.

Vinnie Gold could be suave.

I couldn't help thinking how un-Patsy she had become for a moment there and how unexpected it was. I had been fooled by her once, believing she was as sure of herself as she looked. I knew now how carefully she presented herself to the world, and I knew that she was more afraid than Vincenzo had ever been.

I reached to switch the movie off, but she put a hand on my arm to stop me. "Let's read the names. Maybe some are Italian."

So I waited through the credits, she did the reading. "Is this for a book report?" I asked as the screen went to commercial. "Or maybe you're a movie snob."

She poked me with an elbow and made me grin. Latent violence. But I didn't say anything. I was keeping my thumb on old Vincenzo.

"Can I see your house?" she asked then. "I mean, can I look around?"

"Sure." Full of surprises, that Patsy. But what could I say? She strolled around the living room, touching the pottery and reading the book titles. "I'll dig up something for dessert" was what I came up with while she was riffling through Mr. B's collection of tapes.

I forgot about her for two or three minutes, searching for my mother's private stash of brownies. Just before I found them, I'd convinced myself that Mom had left this habit behind with the apartment. But she'd simply found the ironing closet made a good hiding place.

"I'm going upstairs, okay?" Patsy called.

"Go ahead, I can eat all this by myself," I said, believing she'd come into the kitchen.

But she didn't.

I dished up some ice cream and put a brownie in each bowl. I tried to play it cool and dropped into place on the sofa, but I was up again like it was spring-loaded. Who was I kidding? Had I left that T-shirt next to the phone on my bedside table?

# THIRTY-FOUR

I followed Patsy up the stairs, skipping steps but trying to look casual. Even the sound of my feet was casual.

The lights were on everywhere. She was coming out of the bathroom. "Check the medicine cabinet?" I said. But Patsy was cool.

"Yeah. Nothing incriminating there. I'm on my way to your room."

I went in first, and maybe because she was getting to me, I don't know, I went over and shut the blinds.

"Oh," Patsy said, her tone suggestive. "He likes his privacy." I stayed by the window.

"How about you?" I asked. She let her hand drift over my bookcase, then stopped to play with the photo cube on my desk, turning it over and over to peer at the snapshots.

"Is this you?" she asked, holding the photo cube out to me.

"That's me."

"You were a nerdy-looking little kid."

"That's me."

She laughed, really laughed, and I realized I'd never heard her laugh in person, not this laugh that I'd heard come across the phone wires every so often. It changed her face in a way I liked, made her seem so much more approachable.

She put down the cube, saying, "Me too. Braces, glasses, the works."

"Glasses?"

"I wear contacts. You get good grades, Gold," she said, making one of her lightning-swift shifts to distract me. "You know that, of course."

I didn't say anything about studying to get them. All my better instincts were working overtime, and I let them. For once, thank God, I let them.

She picked up the homework laying on my desk. My strategy for this new English class was to rewrite the essays I'd already gotten good grades on in Queens. But her interest was obviously a ruse to gloss over a moment of vulnerability. Patsy, slightly less than perfect.

"This is pretty interesting. No wonder the teachers are happy about you."

What teachers? I hadn't noticed. "What's so interesting?"

Her eyes narrowed, detecting a whiff of what's-so-interesting-about-me? Patsy turned around to give me the first sheet of several that were paper-clipped together. It read:

My mother reads the daily horoscope in three major New York City papers, one of which requires a neighbor to translate. Mom likes holding the evidence of a large body of believers out there. Three astrologers couldn't be writing for just one small dark-haired woman in a ratty chenille robe. Also, numerical strength effectively destroys any aura of superstition that might scent the air.

"In all fairness," I said—sounding very nearly normal, considering that I had no idea what lie I was about to tell—"the subject was suggested to me. I didn't come up with it by myself."

"You have your own phone?" Patsy said, playing it cool. "A private number, I mean."

I understood the question. The thing was, I didn't want to answer it. I think I was grinning inanely, trying to think of what I could say that would distract her completely. But my mind was a blank. A blank.

Patsy hadn't moved a muscle. Her cheeks pinked up. And then she blushed from the neckline of her sweater right up to the roots of her hair. "You worried about something?" I asked her.

"No." Defensively. She doesn't put up with teasing. Not from Vincenzo. Not from Vinnie Gold.

"My mistake. I thought you looked a little nervous."

She didn't answer right away. Then she said, "If I was

nervous, and I'm not saying I am, what would I have to be nervous about?" Her defenses were fast on their feet and not at all inclined to make mistakes. I wished I could say the same for mine.

"Maybe you aren't used to hanging around a guy's bedroom." I leaned back on the bed, propped myself up on an elbow.

"Maybe I'm not," she said in a casual tone that lost a couple of points for breathlessness. "Maybe I am," she said playfully. Her voice failed on "I am," and ruined the effect. She knew it. I saw it in her eyes.

"Maybe you're not. Maybe that's why you ask so many questions." We were both silent then, but the room was filled with energy. War was being waged.

Her mother's car purred through the driveway at just that moment, declaring a truce. "Aren't you serving dessert, Gold?" Patsy said, and turned on her heel.

I followed her downstairs.

Not more than half a dozen words passed between us as we spooned up the softened ice cream. I don't know what she was thinking about. But I knew she was thinking. I also knew it was hopeless to try to second-guess her. I would just have to be ready for her.

But when the ice cream and brownies were gone, it seemed neither of us could think of anything to say. Which made it a good time to say good night. We gravitated to the back door and stood in the charged place where the warm and cold air exchanged greetings. It wasn't all that late, but it was dark. And really cold. We didn't hurry ourselves, though, there was a funny little gap that needed to be filled.

I said, "Want to go to a movie with me? Say, Wednesday night?"

"Wednesday?"

"The teachers have an administration day on Thursday, remember?"

"No school. I know." Patsy gave me one of those size-you-up looks. "I like that."

"What?"

"You're not playing it cool."

"By Wednesday you could be going with somebody else," I said. Like Biff.

She said, "So. Wednesday. A movie."

Patsy didn't turn to go. We stood there, looking at the frosty glaze that was laying itself over the driveway, at the light burning in her kitchen window. Our eyes met once, accidentally, and we were caught in a kind of I-dare-you stare. I was afraid I would be the first to look away, so I leaned down and touched my lips lightly to hers.

It had a kind of elegance. Not touching except for our lips. "Seemed like a good idea to get that out of the way. Now there's nothing to be nervous about."

"Were you nervous?" Her voice shook ever so slightly.

"First times are always nervous." Vinnie Gold made it sound sophisticated.

"'Night, Vinnie."

It wasn't my imagination. She was trembling too. Of

course, it might've had to do with standing in the cold with only the sweater to keep her warm.

"Yeah. See you tomorrow."

I shut the door as soon as she reached her own back door. The trembling had collected itself dead center in my belly and the muscles were working themselves up to actual spasms. I felt short of breath, my heart was banging against the walls of my chest, like I was standing in a large body of water. You can say what you want. But it was there in the way she looked at Vinnie Gold. He was winning her over.

# THIRTY-FIVE

It was hard to say why I found that idea so unsettling. Whether Vinnie won her affections or Vincenzo had her ear even as we entered college and went on to grad school, I was in a win-win situation here, right?

If things went well on Wednesday evening, I could give her a Valentine's Day card and quit calling. So why did I feel torn? Why did I feel for Vincenzo? Why was I pulling for him as if he would lose something if Vinnie succeeded? And why did I feel Patsy had somehow disappointed us? Me.

I didn't know, but that's how it was.

At midnight, I dialed.

"You could've told me there's no *H* in the Italian alphabet."

"That would have been self-defeating." Very smug, that Vincenzo.

"I know about the others, Leonardo."

"Others?" She sounded like she'd been crying again. Stuffed up. A little alarming, considering I'd just spent a couple of hours with her.

It suddenly occurred to me that she might care more about Biff than I thought. She kissed me, sure, but so what? People kiss other people all the time, they date other people, at least until somebody is going steady with somebody else.

"K, X, and Y, W, too."

"Where are you getting your information?"

"From somebody who just says what's on his mind. It's refreshing." Stuffed up and in a pissy mood.

"You don't say." I wasn't sure which way this conversation was about to go. "Are we going to fight?"

"We don't have to. You could take me to the Valentine's Day dance, Luigi."

"Hasn't Biff asked you?" But I was gentle. I really was.

"That isn't his name. It's what you—"

"I know, I know. The jerk who wouldn't let you out of his car."

"He wouldn't do that again."

"What do you think he does for an encore?"

Click.

Did she have hopes that Biff would turn out to be a great guy? No, it just couldn't be that. She was smarter than that.

I allowed myself one exasperated sigh, then dialed again. "You aren't crying about Biff, are you?" My throat tightened, and I could taste salt on my tongue.

"Stop calling him that."

"Or anybody . . . else, right?"

"I'd tell you, Mario. You know I would."

"I don't find that particularly reassuring." And then I felt a little smile start. "We're skipping to Ms?"

"One letter per call."

"So the tears are for . . ."

"Look, I shouldn't be talk—I should never have said anything about my parents. About the problem they're having."

"I'm an obscene caller. Are we worried about my opinion?"

She said, "I don't think you're, like, a hopeless case."

Ordinarily I might have taken advantage of the chance to tease her, even jog her into hanging up. But I heard this little quaver in her voice. I said, "Thanks."

We gave it a moment. She said, "You haven't done this before, have you?"

"Nope. You're the first."

"And the last?"

"I doubt obscene callers generally find this kind of reception."

"I'm not sure that's the answer I was looking for."

"You mean you're hoping I'll make a career of—?"

"Never mind. I'm not in the mood for the way you twist things around."

"Me? I'm the twister?"

"Your parents are divorced, right?"

"Right."

"So okay, given that you know parents have a life outside of being parents, what do you think of—" She broke off with a little sigh. "You already know. One of them having an affair."

"What do I think of it? Well. It happens." I thought I knew what she wanted to hear and came out with something I thought sounded nearly profound. "Lots of men do this sort of thing—"

"Shut up!"

I did. I should have quit while I was ahead.

"You're wrong. My dad would never—" She began to sob. She didn't even try to hide it. Then she hung up.

I sat in the darkness. Clearly, I was a total jerk. I thought about calling back. Decided against it.

Then I dialed.

"What?" she said through her tears.

"I apologize."

Silence.

"No wisecracks. Just, I'm sorry."

"It's really nice to hear someone say that, Nino."

I wondered if she was thinking of a line from the movie we'd just watched. I had to make out like it meant nothing to me. "Nino, huh? You're making real progress tonight."

If she'd baited a little trap that didn't catch me, she didn't linger over it in disappointment. She said, "You have to tell me if I at least get to the right letter. That's one of our rules, isn't it?"

"It gets easier," I said, not quite ready to go back to being flippant. "About your parents, I mean."

"Is that what happened—"

"Not exactly. But it's hard to know one of the most important people in your life is hurting the other one."

"What do you do?"

"Watch. It has a horrible fascination." My voice thickened and I waited for the tears to retreat. "After a while, you find something else to focus on."

"That's like something one of my friends said. That if she was in love, she didn't pay any attention to what her parents were doing."

"Maybe," I said. "It doesn't always happen that people turn up right when you need them."

"You turned up."

I swear my heart twisted like someone turned a knife in it. It hurt like that. It was strangely good. She had found something in our talks to help her. Me too. We sort of depended on each other. Probably we depended on each other in a way we couldn't if we were dating in the usual way.

The tears were not just an odd sound in my throat. I needed to give it a glib finish. "What you tell me goes no further. Obscene callers are like priests. And of course, my secrets are safe with you."

"You're not funny." She was gentle. Sad. "Thanks, uh . . ."

"I think you can give it a rest till tomorrow." You had to be on your toes with Patsy.

"It makes me feel better just to hear your voice."

"I guess the thing to do next time I'm feeling obnoxious is, don't say anything," I said, teasing her.

Patsy sniffled and said, "Can I have your phone number?"

Tears hung suspended from my eyelashes. The effect was peculiar, like looking at everything from underwater. I could even feel the pressure on my chest. "Patsy—"

"I need to talk to you sometimes."

"I'll call you more often." My chest ached with the need to come up for air.

"Sometimes I need to call you." I could hardly hear her. I thought sound traveled so well underwater.

"I can't give you my number." This came out with a muted, garbled sound, like the escape of air bubbles. And I thought I heard her say "please." "I would if I could."

"But you won't." Her voice went flat, cold.

"Can't," I pleaded. "It's different."

"Not to me, it isn't."

"You know why that is?" I was angry all of a sudden. "You don't see me as a person who lives twenty-three-and-a-half hours a day after I talk to you. You never think what these calls mean to me. Or what it might mean if you knew who I am. You just talk until you've said what you want to say, and if I'm not telling you what you want to hear—"

Click.

—you just hang up.

I guess I made my point.

# THIRTY-SIX

Something she said really got to me, I guess. I could hardly sleep. I watched the clock record the passing of minutes. I dozed awhile, then woke to stare at the clock again.

I really wanted to be Patsy's friend, not just over the phone, but sitting in class, standing in line in the cafeteria, riding the bus. I wanted Patsy to want me, Vinnie Gold, to give her a valentine. But I remember a conversation my parents had once when they were still getting along, still loved each other the way they were supposed to.

I was maybe ten, and they were just talking when my mom said, "Remember Paul?" and they both laughed. It was a little bit mean-sounding.

My impression was, Paul was a real clown. Which was what I called a jerk back then. So I asked, "Who's Paul?"

And Mom said, "I dated him in high school."

"You guys didn't go to high school together, did you?" I was pretty sure. Mom was from Long Island and Dad was from Milwaukee.

"No, no," Dad said. "But your mom told me about all her guys. I told her about all my girls."

I was ten, so I shrugged, but it made an impression on me. And what I knew now, no matter what happened between me and Patsy from here on out, once she knew it was me making these calls, I would, someday far in the future, be the guy she remembered as someone who loved her, yeah— but what a clown.

I really didn't want to be that guy.

And now it was too late to be any other.

The next morning I did just what Patsy asked, true to my word. I told Mr. B that she needed Italian names for an assignment. But he didn't know that many Italian names.

"Let's see. I had an uncle named Salvatore. My brother was named after our father, Roberto."

Left to his own devices, he'd made breakfast—bread with a circle cut out of it and fried with an egg dropped into the empty circle.

"You can cook?"

"Sure, I cook," he said. "I've been a bachelor a long time. But in my mother's house, the wife cooked. And your mom was so excited about the kitchen, I thought she must love cooking. So I stopped when I got married."

"Till this morning," I said.

"I like eating," Mr. B said. "Breakfast especially. Donuts are okay, but I need something to keep the chill off when I'm standing on that field. I need hot food."

"Looks great."

"There's plenty here for all of us," he said.

"So. Names?" I handed him two plates.

"There's, uh, Mario and Giuseppe and Giovanni. You think that's enough?"

"Sure. How many could she need?"

"What are you two talking about?" Mom asked as she whisked into the kitchen for a glass of juice.

Mr. B was still in pajamas. I was in my sweats, but I'd taken to sleeping in the ones I'd wear the next morning, so in a way, I was in pajamas too. Mom was already dressed for work, a little tornado of energy.

"The neighbor girl needs some Italian names for some project or other," Mr. B answered, shrugging.

Packing her little travel bag with heels, appointment book, her purse, and the red thermos, Mom said, "Sounds like the project is to get closer to you, Vinnie."

Actually, I'd meant to tell them I had a date with Patsy on Wednesday, but it felt weird now. Really weird. "I hardly know her," I said, dipping into the cereal box I'd been munching from.

"That's what I mean." Mom noticed what I was doing. "Don't eat standing up. And don't eat straight out of the box."

Mr. B set the plates on the table, where sliced tomatoes lay on a small cutting board. "Hungry?" he asked her.

"Not yet. I'll get something at work."

I sat down across from Mr. B, who forked a tomato slice onto the top of my egg and toast. He said, "I don't see you making any friends, Vinnie. Are you getting along okay?"

"Fine," I said, attacking my meal with knife and fork.

"Who've you been hanging around with?"

"Nobody in particular," I said around the first delectable bite.

"Out of particular, then," Mr. B said with a note of real concern.

Mom said, "Dom—"

"I've gotten to know a few kids," I said quickly. "Just nobody I want to hang around with."

"How about girls?"

"Dom!"

I stood up, downing the rest of the egg and half the fried bread in two quickly swallowed bites. "I'll get around to girls," I said as I dragged on my backpack. "I'm heading out for my run."

"I'll drive you to school," Mr. B said, rising from the table.

"No. No. I'm still working up to being seen on the track."

But I'd eaten too fast and my energy drained away as I jogged to the end of the block. I walked toward the bus stop. I saw Patsy there, and then I saw Biff coast up to the corner from the other side of the block.

The girls walked over to the car and talked to him for a minute. Even Patsy. Clearly, she had accepted an apology for Biff's behavior. Did that mean she'd accept mine?

After a minute, she got into the car with him and he drove off. I could hardly believe my eyes. Okay, they were headed in the direction of the school. But he was history. Wasn't he history? Does attempted rape get a second chance? Why didn't she get *him* to find her some Italian names if she thought he was so terrific?

I couldn't make myself go stand and wait for the bus and have to listen while Brown Bunny commented on this turn of events. I headed back the other way. Steamed, I kept on walking in the wrong direction.

When I turned around, I was already late to school. I ran one block, then walked one. My throat didn't burn, but I couldn't expect to win a race if I couldn't run much farther than a block. It occurred to me that I might have chosen the wrong sport.

If I didn't regret my commitment to become a track star enough, Mr. B had singled me out for some special attention, even though I missed half the class. He nodded to me approvingly several times, the way he does with his football team. I felt like a complete fake.

Sometimes you can't win for losing.

Biff was in the locker room afterward. He was in some mood, talking about putting the wow on some girl. I'd already sneered at the dance posters on the way to class, and what he had to say held no interest for me.

But he had a willing audience in the guys standing around the locker room. They received his next line with an encouraging nod of their heads, and several slaps to the arms.

"So I put a hand on her shoulder in this fatherly way, ya know how I mean, and I brought her up real close, and I said, 'I really like you, Patsy, better than any girl I ever knew.' She was eating it up, I swear, and I let my hand drift."

Anticipatory moans urged him on.

"I was thinking I'd have to sit like that for a while to get her used to it"—ol' Biff wasn't one to be rushed through a story he was enjoying so much—"but when I moved in to kiss her, she about swooned—"

I can't stand guys who do this. I really can't. But mostly I couldn't stand listening to Biff do this. I wanted to be the one to say those things to Patsy, do those things with Patsy. Not under the exact same circumstances, of course, but I wanted to be the one. So sue me.

"I went ahead and slid my hand right onto her boob. It did her in, man! I mean, she was so . . ."

I slammed my locker door, interrupting the party for a split second. Then their heads swiveled back to ol' Biff. "She's such a babe, you know, just ripe for it—"

Girls haven't been that uneducated since the Middle Ages. If then. "You're a real jerk, you know that?" I said.

"Huh?"

That was Biff, but even I could hardly believe what I said. There was nothing to do but follow up. "Some guys talk like that before they've done it. And then either they grow up or they keep on talking about the girls who are nice to them because *they* have a problem. So which one are you?"

Right then, I was aware that all eyes were on me. It was as if my peripheral vision had widened to take in all the amazed faces. And I don't think it was my imagination that some of those faces wore a sheepish expression. Not one of Biff's avid listeners believed a word he said. Which was not to say they weren't happy to listen and repeat every word to anyone who'd missed show time. The other thing that hit me, I had instinctively chosen the one accusation guaranteed to get under Biff's skin.

But all that took a heartbeat. And that was all I had.

I don't think he knocked me out, but I don't remember hitting the floor. I just remember opening my eyes and going on talking. "No guy worth shit talks—"

He was right on me and knocked the breath out of me, but I kept on talking whenever I could put words together.

"...about a girl...like that...Probably she... wouldn't..."

I was crying, but I didn't realize it at the time. I hardly even noticed Biff pounding on me. All I saw was his stupid face in front of me like a red moon and this sound, something roaring all around us. Then somebody grabbed him off me.

# THIRTY-SEVEN

Later, somebody told me it took several guys to grab Biff off me, Mr. B among them. Biff and I spent most of the day in the dean's office while everybody gave their version of what happened.

Mr. B was in the dean's office a lot of that time so I know that two lines, often repeated, sealed Biff's fate. One, that he was saying some pretty coarse stuff about one of the girls, and two, that although I'd called him on it, I'd never lifted a hand to fight.

While I wouldn't have counted that last thing as a point in my favor, it seemed to work for me here. Biff got three days in-school suspension and a warning that any further disruption would make him ineligible for sports.

He hadn't succeeded in killing me—that point worked in his favor. And Mr. B still had his star player.

I had a fat lip the nurse treated with ice, and an assortment of lumps and bruises on my head and shoulders that were vaguely purple. But except to say that I could expect some swelling, medical science didn't have much to offer.

Neither did the dean. He said a few things like he knew I really applied myself to my academic subjects, and it seemed to him that I was going to be an outstanding student. It didn't hurt that the dean was the track coach. Mr. B must have put in a good word for me, because the dean knew I was going out for the team in the spring. He said he always finds his best men in the long-and-lean types, like me, and he clapped me on the back.

I was okay in his book, that was it, just one of the guys, and with high principles besides. He said I would also have to apply myself to keeping out of trouble, but he said it with this embarrassed expression that meant he believed I'd done something vaguely admirable in any case and he didn't want to come down too hard on me.

I was right to want Mr. B to like me. He'd had a lot to do with the attitude the dean was taking, I was sure. But I left the office with an odd nagging feeling that I'd sold out. I'd let the dean think I was one of them.

A jock.

Practically all the principals and the superintendents are. My mom pointed this out once, before she married one. When you get them talking, they tell you how in their early teaching careers, right up until they reached higher administration, they were the proud coaches of this team or that. They talk about it with a glistening eye that turns cloudy when you ask how they feel about accelerated education.

I didn't want to take the bus home. I decided to run.

It was rough, more so because I was pushing it, wanting the run to be over. I kept going till I nearly vomited, slowed to a walk for several blocks, then ran again, slower.

Patsy was hanging around her front yard as I jogged down the street, making me glad I'd set it up so I looked good on the home stretch. I was conscious of the ugly puffiness under one eye, and of a swollen lower lip that sported my own tooth marks. I hoped it was merely coincidental that she was outside. I didn't want to talk about Italian anything. But she walked over to meet me.

"Hey, wait up," she called as I passed her by. I kept going, but she ran alongside as I came up the driveway. "You look awful."

"Thanks."

"I don't mean it like that." Breathe, breathe. "Did he hurt you much?"

I slowed to a walk. "Not much."

"I'm sorry."

"Why are *you* apologizing?"

"It's just . . . he was my boyfriend and all."

I clenched my teeth over the question I wanted to ask: *Is that what you're calling him now?*

"You didn't know?"

"Nope," I said as I reached the house.

I shut the back door behind me. Did I know he was boy-friend material? No, I didn't. Vincenzo knew, of course, but not me. I was the dumbbell who'd asked her out for Wednesday night. I wasn't even sure we were still on.

She knocked.

Disbelieving, I opened up. "What is it?" *Now*, my tone implied.

"What did you fight about?"

"It was his fight. Why don't you ask him?"

"I just wondered why he hit you."

"You're talking to the wrong guy," I said as I shut the door on her again. It hit me halfway up the stairs. I'd hung up.

To top it all off, Dad called. I wouldn't have minded so much if I was doing victory laps, but . . . I wasn't.

"Mom tells me you got into a fight."

"I didn't know you talked to her," I said, but a lot of things I didn't know instantly came clear. Mr. B had called Mom at her office, and of course that's when she called Dad, probably before I got through third period.

Dad was saying, "When did we ever stop talking to each other? Besides, we still have you."

"It wasn't much of a fight. He hit me. I fell down."

"Why'd he hit you?"

"Mistaken identity."

"Mistaken for who?"

"Somebody who'd fight back."

"Yeah, your mom said he'll be doing time."

"It's not a life sentence, I'm sorry to report."

We talked for a while, Dad going through his latest funny taxi driver stories, before we said good-bye.

I still had to put on a good face for my mother when she got home. Easier said than done, considering the swelling under my eye.

"Dom, is that permanent?" This was her "hide your horror" voice, but fear was still there, in her eyes. It was kind of gratifying, if you want to know the truth.

"Of course not."

Mom rounded on Mr. B. "You said it was nothing. He looks like Marlon Brando as a waterfront rat."

I don't think Mr. B got the movie reference. Or maybe he was caught between building me up to feel like I'd stormed the battlements and the more subdued story he'd told her.

Me, I was surprised she wasn't cooler about the whole thing. It suddenly occurred to me that while Mom had appeared to take a "no skin off my nose" attitude to my pinched finger, she probably felt responsible she hadn't avoided the accident somehow. She'd probably downplayed her own anxieties when she was with me.

Because now Mom was talking like they ought to pack me off to the emergency room. "Or we can drive into Queens and see Dr. Saltzman. He'll squeeze us in before he goes home for the night."

"We're not going anywhere," I said, imitating the way Mr. B had once spoken over a gasping body lying on the gym floor. He'd gotten down on one knee, popped a dislocated shoulder back into place, and sent everybody else back to a volleyball game with a reminder of each team's scores. "I don't even have a loose tooth."

"I didn't even think of his teeth. Have you looked, Dom?"

"I looked. Nothing chipped. I don't think he needs a doctor," he told Mom.

If her first reaction could be described as barely controlled hysteria, as the evening went on, her later reaction was made up of two parts "what might have happened" and one part "this wouldn't have happened if we'd stayed in the city, where we belong."

I was quick to remind her that I'd had my share of difficulty in the city, and asked if she remembered tripping over my self-defense books for weeks after the mugging. It seemed she'd forgotten how strongly that episode had figured in the move to Long Island.

Mr. B called the swelling "a mouse," and after we ate the manicotti dinners he'd brought home with him, he said I ought to go up to my room and grab a nap.

I slept through most of the evening, waking up at ten-thirty to start homework. Right then, I turned the dial on the alarm clock and bought myself an extra hour of sleep in the morning.

Running. Who needed it?

# THIRTY-EIGHT

I almost skipped the call. To be frank, I didn't like Patsy quite so much tonight. And we'd had enough face-to-face conversations at this point that I had begun to worry she'd know my voice.

Only I had to call that night. To cover myself.

And then I'd see.

"Orlando!"

"Good name."

"And?"

"That's all. Just not bad as names go."

"I thought I had you today."

"Had me where?"

"Don't be like that. I thought *you* fought for my honor."

"I heard about it. That's about as close as I got to your honor."

"It was a guy who lives next door to me. When I asked him why he got into a fight, I said it was my boyfriend that hit him."

"You called Biff your boyfriend?" I made my voice incredulous, not hard to do. "Don't you think you're being awfully forgiving here?"

"That's not his name, but you see what I mean? This guy next door didn't bat an eyelash at the word 'boyfriend.' That's when I figured out he wasn't you."

I still didn't know why she got into his car this morning, but I was pretty sure he must have been singing a different song than in the locker room. I decided to let it go.

"Disappointed?" I asked her.

"In what way?"

"That the other guy wasn't me? Maybe I was part of the audience Biff was sounding off for," I said. "I may have been standing there with the other half a dozen guys—"

"Don't be disgusting."

I had gotten a little carried away. Actually, I'd discovered it wasn't so much that I didn't like her. I was angry with her. It had to do with the things Biff said, sure, but I didn't blame her for that.

I blamed her for getting into his car again.

I blamed her for giving the guy a second chance. Even though our calls were happening only because she gave me one.

I waited for her to hang up.

What I liked, she ignored the whole outburst. She went

on as if I'd swallowed something the wrong way and she'd been interrupted to pat me on the back. You had to admire her style.

"So it's true. He was talking about me." Annoyed now. "And you do see me in school. You're close to me every day, I think I knew that. Sometimes you're mad at me before you call. Sometimes," she said, "you sound like you don't like me very much."

"I like you," I said, knowing I sounded like a drowning man who chooses between the call for help or a lungful of air before he sinks again. "I do." Nothing from her. "Sometimes I say things, I don't always know why. It doesn't mean anything."

I caught myself there, groveling.

"We could be friends," she said. "You could meet me at the dance."

"We could be *better* friends if you'd decide these calls are enough for you."

"I don't know that we could," she said, and hung up.

The truth was, I hadn't handled the whole conversation very well. I got angry, and then I gave myself away. A little detective work and she could narrow down her list of suspects to maybe a dozen guys. Including me.

I thought about calling back to apologize. After all, what was she asking for? To get to know me in person. That's what this was all about at the beginning. Right? Okay, it would be a little awkward at first. Vinnie Gold, acting like he's so cool.

She might even be angry with me for the deception. I didn't believe that would last. I'd admitted to being someone she would recognize. Vinnie Gold, fool for love.

It was my impression that she stood behind what she said. She could accept the worst. Vinnie Gold, remember that clown?

I didn't feel up to dialing.

If you want to know the truth, I was beginning to feel a kind of battle fatigue. Even when I was winning, it felt like losing.

I couldn't get up the next morning. I kept pushing the snooze button on my alarm clock. It tried to get me up every nine minutes. I didn't get up until ten minutes before the bus was due.

"Vinnie. I thought you'd gone."

"I'm going. Bye, Mom."

"Vin—"

Maybe I ran on nervous energy, I don't know, but I moved at a dead sprint. The only good thing was, it was really nippy this morning. Every time I felt dizzy, I sucked in a strong, deep breath of frozen air, and when I reached the bus stop, I had the idea I didn't look half bad. I got there just as kids were boarding, my chest heaving, ears threatening to explode with the pressure in my head.

I headed for a seat in the back, acting as if I'd never seen Patsy. And Biff? He got on the bus at the next stop. The seat next to Patsy was already taken, and he had to sit two rows behind her. Which meant nothing, really. Yesterday morning she got into his car.

What I would have liked to see, him taking the seat next to her and Patsy finding someplace else to sit.

I went into the school through the door the teams used after morning warm-ups. I'd never used it before, and I wanted to feel more familiar with this part of the building. It led down a short strip of hallway with double doors to the locker rooms and ended at the gym. I stopped in the boys' locker room to wait for the bell, which rang moments later.

The teams came in like a herd of thundering buffalo, capable of mowing down anything standing in their way. Me, for instance. But it was a cheerful herd, and as the guys passed the showers, they broke almost immediately into a not-quite-orderly division into the locker rows, sparing my life.

I sat down on the bench in front of my locker. I was light-headed, probably from lack of food. My injuries weren't particularly impressive—even the black eye looked like a practical joke. Thanks to the puffiness that appeared around my jawline overnight, I looked petulant rather than battered.

A few guys looked at me as if they'd never seen me before, more of them grinned to let me know they'd decided I was okay.

Biff came in from the other set of double doors, signaling he'd come through the front of the school. This was clearly a demotion. Why he'd come here was anybody's guess, probably it just felt strange that his first whiff of school was of straight floor wax without the buffer of sweaty socks.

Anyone on a team was there in the locker room, of course. Guys said hello to Biff, but no one encouraged him to brag more. They acted like all they had on their minds was a speedy shower, dragging on their clothing, and combing wet hair.

I gathered Mr. B had given them quite the lecture about disrespecting girls, and then a hefty after-school cleaning assignment to underline his disappointment in them. So it was understandable Biff wasn't being met with a friendly razzing.

Biff strode right to his locker without speaking to anyone. He didn't look in my direction, and he didn't look like he anticipated a good day. That worked for me. I left before the start-of-day bell rang.

# THIRTY-NINE

In the hallways, it seemed to me several girls offered me shy glances and sweet smiles. Chivalry was not dead.

There was a sharper sort of appraisal in the teachers' eyes, even though it seemed unlikely that a locker room fracas could merit a prime-time airing in the teachers' lounge.

Brown Bunny came up to me between classes late in the afternoon. "You're something of a hero," she said. She used a tone I couldn't read.

She'd already struck me as one of those playground bullies, the one that threw sand in your eyes when nobody's mother was looking. I never could figure out how that kid timed things so perfectly, again and again. I said nothing.

"You've got potential," she said to me.

"As what?"

"I'm not dating anyone currently."

"Really? I thought you were." He was kind of a hoody type, but he was able to cross the line between the hoody kids and the popular kids without any problem that I could see. I didn't know if Brown Bunny was his hall pass or if he was, in some weird alternative universe, hers.

She let this exchange just hang there between us. Was she telling me she'd be more interested in dating me?

She was terrifying.

"I'm not dating anyone either," I said, grateful to hear the bell ring. I turned to go into my next classroom, hearing the musical theme from *Jaws* retreat as I put some distance between us.

I headed out to the track after school. I hadn't made any announcement that I had an interest in the team or anything, but I was out there with them. I warmed up and started around the track.

Biff was out there too. He couldn't work out with the football team until he was off suspension, but Mr. B made sure he could use the track. I could see why Mr. B had been so adamant. It wasn't just punishment. Biff didn't run, he lumbered. Oh, not that he was hopeless, but I was caught up in the poetry of it.

He tried not to notice me as I came up behind him. He tried to stay even. He was blowing like an old horse as I passed him. Not that I was going to win an award. We weren't alone on the track, and there were runners passing both of us. There were runners passing those runners.

Once I was past him, he was not on my radar. I was too busy noticing that while I wasn't especially fast, I also wasn't straining, which surprised me. I was actually enjoying myself.

11:59. I'd been thinking over my relationship with Patsy. I wondered if it wasn't so much guarded as it was phobic.

I had to think about this from another angle. Had I developed a genuine split personality? I mean, by day I was the boy next door, kinda funny, kinda smart, but not stopping traffic in the halls between classes. I cringed at the idea of Patsy rejecting me. For a few minutes every night, Vincenzo extracted a price for that. He made her pay, if only in uncertainty.

That's what I was thinking as I dialed.

She opened with a formal tone. "You remember there's a Valentine's Day dance coming up at school, Paolo." Like we hadn't touched on this subject before.

Playing along, I said, "I've seen the posters."

There had to be twenty of them up in the halls. The dance committee had gone wild with hearts and lace and scarlet eye masks.

"Are you going?"

"I don't dance," I lied.

"Everyone dances. It's not like you have to remember any steps," she said, dismissing that argument.

"Not me."

"We could meet at the dance, you know," she said.

"I guess I'll be the wallflower who spends all his time in the line for soda. Yellow mask, don't you think?"

"You have to take risks, Patrizio," she said in this terribly crisp tone of voice. "To be a survivor, you have to take risks and"—she paused—"and survive."

"This is the advice you're offering an obscene caller?"

"What if I guessed who you are? What's the worst thing that could happen?"

"You've got to be kidding." There were warning bells going off all through my nervous system. I didn't have time to analyze the reaction, but I sat there with it just long enough for her to sense my resistance.

"Tell me *something*," she said, very definite. She'd found some inequity in the rules. "Something that won't give you away, Pietro. Something personal?"

"I told you about my dad."

"You know my mom is having an affair. You know much more about me all around."

"That's your theory." I was catching a wave. "What if I've only been making good guesses? What if I don't actually know who you are?"

"Will you ever tell me who you are? Am I ever going to be someone you care that much about? Because I think I know you. I think I probably talk to you every day."

"You've got a lot of questions for a girl who doesn't notice somebody she talks to every day," I said, just as if my insides hadn't started quivering like a bowstring. I sounded strong.

"What if I gave you a question in return?"

"You wouldn't like my questions. You wouldn't answer my questions."

"Maybe I won't even answer the phone," she said.

I didn't respond, hoping she'd hang up.

"I think you're going to be at the dance." Patsy the terrier. "Couples have to go as romantic couples, you know. From movies or literature."

"Are you going as a couple?" I asked.

"I'm going by myself."

"A single woman. So will it be a glamour choice?" I asked her, adopting a flirty tone. "Princess Leia. Or forbidden romance. The little schoolmarm in *Butch Cassidy and the Sundance Kid*."

"I don't know who I think is romantic," she said wearily, signaling defeat. "I'll just wear a mask."

"A girl's mask. Something sequined and feline. Your hair hidden under a Marie Antoinette wig."

"Do you like my hair?"

It killed me the way she asked it. She could've been simpering or teasing, very sure of herself. But she wasn't. She had a little-girl voice that only wanted to know if this guy who wouldn't meet her at the dance at least liked her hair. I never expected that from her.

"Yes," I croaked. Her frog prince. "I like your hair."

"Are Italians drawn to blondes, do you think, because they're so dark?" She could bounce right back, Patsy could.

"Northern Italians aren't necessarily dark."

"So I'll see you at the dance, Peppino?" she asked.

"You'll have Biff drive you?"

"I'm going to ignore that."

The terrible thing, as we hung up, I was tempted to call back and say *Yes, let's meet at the dance*. Really tempted. We weren't even getting along all that well and I wanted to do what she wanted me to do.

How strange could I get?

# FORTY

Mr. B wanted eggs, and no doubt he'd have cooked them himself, but there weren't any. Also, he liked Italian bread and Mom chose whatever looked healthiest to her. This week's choice tasted like stale graham crackers, and if asked, I would've agreed with him. He made the coffee, as usual, and Mom had all she needed.

Mr. B made me take a few bucks to buy breakfast at a little corner store, and I left without weighing in on the debate. I was buoyed up with anticipating the fried ham and egg sandwich they made at that place.

I wasn't cold once I started running, and my body didn't protest so much, but until I got out there, my mind put up a lot of resistance. *Why are you punishing yourself?* it asked me. *What kind of accomplishment is this?*

But I fell into something like my run-one-block, walk-one-block rhythm. I ran a little longer at a stretch. The walking breaks were shorter. There was hope.

I tried running slower. Maybe my lungs would hold up better. Trying it, I decided the idea had merit. Speed could be built up after I could run a distance without pain. Couldn't it?

As I savored the ham and egg sandwich, I reviewed the run. Overall, I ran better. By the time I got to school, I felt up to jogging around the track a couple of times.

Biff was out there again, but I ignored him. I ran easily, I ran focused, and for maybe a minute, I ran fast. When the dean showed up, Biff left the track and sat out the next couple of laps on the bleachers.

But the dean didn't have Biff on his radar screen. He only wanted to jog around the track a few times himself. Good for the old heart, like he said. Good for mine too, because he was demonstrating that all running isn't done at breakneck speed.

He introduced me to a couple of the guys on his team as they trotted past. That's how he put it, "his team," and in making the introductions he didn't tell them I was hoping to qualify. He didn't say anything to put me on the spot.

It didn't bother me that the dean was talking to me like I was a jock, like he didn't know I was one of his better students and probably had never made a team. It was good he did most of the talking, but I was able to keep up with him as we jogged around the track. I was feeling pretty good.

The bell rang and everyone headed for the locker room—

another chorus of pounding heels. Biff was not in the lead. I discovered the tides were shifting for him, which, when I got around to thinking about it, might mean he had other things to worry about besides my gaining popularity with Mr. B.

"Hey, let's have a look at the love letter, huh?"

There was some heavy backslapping going on. Odd that Biff didn't look all that pleased.

"Yeah, you guys heard about the love letter our star player received this morning? No?" the team's running back asked. His towel cracked like a whip and just missed taking the eye of an innocent bystander seated between Biff and myself. Said bystander went unfazed, being quite the towel-snapper himself, and joined in with his own brand of witty repartee.

He nudged Biff. "Been keeping it very much to yourself, huh?"

I kept my head down, eyes on my locker. But I hated that she'd sent him a note. I wanted to get off by myself and think. Last night we'd talked about the dance. Had she hinted that she and Biff weren't over? Had my refusal sent her in his direction?

"One of those Chinese folds the girls are always doing," the towel-cracker added informatively. "You could use it like a paper cup, but you have to know the secret of the fold to be able to read it without tearing it up. Guess he knows the secret."

Ol' Biff kept strictly silent, which was strictly out of character. But they didn't leave it alone.

"Must be love letters are private, wouldn't you say?" Snap.

"How would I know? How many love letters do you see me getting, huh?"

Mr. B walked into the locker room then, and everyone settled down. Biff was off the hook, though. He hadn't responded to the towel-snapper and he certainly hadn't added to the general merriment. He finished changing and left without saying a word. Hard to figure the Biffs in this world.

Patsy just happened to be hanging out in the hallway as I left the locker room.

My heart lifted a little. She had her next class with me, and I was fairly certain that Biff's next class was in the shop wing, in the other direction. So I wasn't entirely surprised when she came up to me.

And yet I quickly looked for a Chinese fold—I couldn't even say why. Simply that I'd just heard about it and I had no idea what to expect from her, I guess.

But while I dealt with hope mixed with a kind of dread, I think I came off as if Vinnie Gold takes this kind of thing in stride, if girls hadn't always been waiting in the hall, hoping to walk to class with him, it had only been a matter of time. Vinnie Gold couldn't be overeager, and I let Patsy carry the conversational ball.

"I guess you'll be on the track team," she said.

"I guess."

"Are we still on for the movie?"

"You don't still have a boyfriend?"

She didn't even flinch. "Ex-boyfriend. I didn't really have one on Sunday, either. I should have made myself clearer."

The implication being that she should've been clearer with me, but I wasn't sure that was the whole truth. Not that I cared at just that moment. "We're on for the movie," I said.

"What time?"

"I'll pick you up at five-thirty. It's a walk." I was a little embarrassed to have to be asked what time I was picking her up, but not mortified. Maybe Vinnie was so cool, he wasn't into details.

What Vincenzo did, Vincenzo took note that on the other side of the corridor, Biff and two of his buddies were watching him with Patsy, one of the buddies jubilantly poking Biff in the ribs. Some buddies.

I was staring certain death in the eye—damned if you do and damned if you don't—and I suppose that had something to do with my attitude. I glanced once more at Biff's blood pressure gauge as Patsy started walking, and I turned to follow her.

I was kind of dazed. We were halfway to class, talking about the homework, before I thought of this: Patsy waiting for me in the hall meant the Chinese fold had been a breakup note.

Certain death.

I was in the middle of the morning before I noticed my head didn't hurt. My throat wasn't raw. My legs didn't shiver with the bending of a knee, dropping me suddenly into my desk from a half-seated position.

I saw Biff again in print shop, but he was genuinely busy

there, and reduced to glaring at me in an ugly way when our eyes happened to meet. But now I'd had time to devote to thinking things over. Biff was in a tough spot, Biff was. He had suffered public humiliation when Vinnie Gold had defended Biff's "woman," and his problem now would be how to regain his lost standing.

The answer seemed to be obvious to Biff, I felt sure, but he had to keep his paws off me to stay on the team. Short of satisfaction, he would want revenge, and however lacking in subtlety it might be, it would be likely to take a dangerous form.

I didn't need confirmation on this, but it came later that day. Biff caught me coming out of the restroom outside the locker room. As in, he filled the doorway before I exited.

He was standing right up next to me now, shirt button to shirt button. A kind of survival instinct made me stand my ground, even though he smelled strongly of garlic.

He poked me in the chest a couple of times, the kind of rough stuff a football hero thinks is playful. "You probably think I wouldn't lay a hand on you again," he said, like it was a joke or something. "Me bein' your stepdaddy's star football player."

To tell you the truth, this surprised me. I hadn't really considered ol' Biff to be someone with powers of perception. It hadn't occurred to me that while I was figuring him out, he might be figuring me out. That was rule number one in all those self-defense books: Don't underestimate the enemy.

"But it don't really matter to me they make me ineligible," Biff was saying. "I got no use for being pounded to death, and I don't need to sweat the grades, either."

This statement had a certain logic, but Biff lacked sincerity. He'd want to stay on the team so he'd get to pound somebody *else* to death. He'd only established that we both had something to lose.

Him, the football hero label. Me, my life.

Then somebody else wanted to come into the restroom, making the point by hitting Biff on the back of the head. He snarled and cleared the doorway.

I called Dad. Mona answered.

"I've got an audition for a Pillsbury commercial. I'm a runner-up."

"Hey, cool." It really was. Runner-ups had been through a couple of auditions already and had beaten the competition. I wondered how many other runner-ups there were, but I knew better than to ask. She was probably a bundle of nerves. "Keeping my fingers crossed, Mona."

She called Dad to the phone.

I had to ask myself, was she the date? Nah. She was practically family. She'd come to our house on Mom's invitation first, an actress doing office work to pay her rent. She sort of straddled the friendship line there—lots in common with

Dad, but she and Mom shared the deepest of secrets, office gossip.

"Hi, Vinnie," Dad said, coming on the phone with a hollow sound to his casual manner. "What's doing?"

"Got company?"

There was a pause, then: "We're working on Mona's audition, but I can talk."

Mona? Or maybe he didn't want to talk about a date while Mona was listening in. I read him some of the instruction manual we'd picked up at the aquarium shop, mainly because it was something he was familiar with. It was my opener.

We didn't talk anything but fish tank until the last few seconds of the call. I felt his embarrassment that there were things unsaid—heard it in his voice somehow, I guess, while he talked salt levels—and it was enough to know he was. Embarrassed, I mean.

"It's okay, Dad. The instructions cover a lot of this."

He said, "Well, Mona's waiting."

He said, "Hey, how about next week I'll come out and we'll take in a movie? A movie and a couple of hot dogs, okay?"

"Tuesday night," I said because it used to be our regular night when Mom and I were still in Forest Hills. Only as I got off the phone, I realized I'd forgotten all about asking his advice on my problem with Biff.

# FORTY-ONE

Vinnie Gold dressed carefully. Pants a trifle snug. Black turtleneck under a heavy cotton shirt. A non-puffy jacket Mom found on sale. Vinnie Gold did a few dance steps across his bedroom. Very Bob Fosse. Patsy would know she'd been out with Mr. Cool.

Patsy must have been watching for me. She came out as I started up her walk. I stopped and waited for her, deciding that was how Vinnie handled things. She wore the latest Bloomingdale's look for the suburbs, one my mother kept looking at in the catalog—probably called "Scarsdale Winter" or something. White pants, white sweater, white boots. She looked great.

I didn't know what we'd talk about, exactly.

But Patsy got the ball rolling. Her questions had questions and I answered them carefully, disclosing only the facts that made Vinnie Gold a stronger character. Vinnie Gold never worried about whether he made a good impression, never wondered if he had done the right thing. He was sure of himself. And when the time seemed right, he had a few questions himself.

By the time we reached the cinema, I knew every major event of her life, up to and including sixth grade. When we came back out it was dark, and we weren't dressed warmly enough to fight the cold. We ducked into a diner for hot chocolate. I expected she'd fill me in from seventh grade up to the present, but she wanted to know more about me. She asked whether I'd left anyone pining for me on the isle of Manhattan.

All right, Vinnie Gold came from New York and she assumed Manhattan. Anyway, I said my girlfriend had moved away a few weeks before my mother made a decision to remarry. I made it that we'd accepted the inevitable and broken off our relationship completely. I made it tragic. It seemed like a good time to ask the question that burned beneath my tongue.

"Tell me what happened between you and your boy-friend."

"We dated, that's all," she said.

"You made it sound like something more."

"I hoped he'd turn out to be somebody I liked, but he didn't," she said, evading the question about the boyfriend label. "I gave it a chance, I went out with him a couple of times."

"He's a big-deal sports hero."

"I know. That's why I gave it a chance."

Vinnie Gold wasn't touched by this admission, but somewhere, deep inside, Vincenzo was trembling with emotion.

"Okay, he wasn't making your heart throb. Why break it off?"

She shrugged. "He's . . . pushy. He doesn't take no for an answer."

"So why me?" I asked.

"Why am I going out with you?"

"I think I'm an excellent choice," Vinnie Gold said with a disarming smile. "What I want to hear are your reasons."

"You're not popular in the sense that everyone knows you," she said frankly. "But you've made an impression around school."

Vinnie Gold ought to like flattery. But it was making Vincenzo antsy. She might be working up to me asking her to the dance. "We'd better get going," I said. "While we're feeling warmed up."

But the wind snatched away our stored-up heat before we'd gone a hundred feet. We were crossing the street when a vision appeared. "Look," I cried as my arm shot up into the air. "Taxi!"

It swerved in our direction. I grabbed Patsy around the shoulders and ran. "Will you take us home?" I yelled, bent over to send my voice through the partially open window.

"You on your way to the city, Bud?"

"No. We're on your way, though. You don't have to start the meter."

"How far?"

"Couple of miles."

"Five bucks."

"Done." Patsy and I fell into the backseat, shivering. At least it was a heated cab. I'd had to let go of her to get into the taxi, but I planned to recapture the territory.

However, she was leaning eagerly over the front seat. "Is your name Italian? Aldo, I mean."

"Yeah," he said, his tone guarded and ready to take offense.

"Oh, great, do you know any others?"

"Other what?" he said, like he didn't believe his ears.

"Italian names are so sexy, my friends and I have decided to give our children Italian names." Pretty sly, that Patsy. "Mainly the boys. We're making a list."

He laughed, relaxing then. She was playing the giddy teenager, and he was buying it. "Let's see, there's Mario and Bartolo—"

"How about from the end of the alphabet?" she asked, rooting through her purse for a pen.

"Where we going, Bud?"

"Straight ahead six blocks and a right turn."

"Right. Umberto and Ugo and Tino and . . ." I settled into the corner, with one arm stretched behind Patsy in case she should sit back. Then I just watched her getting wound up over the names she'd never thought of. It was fun to see her excited—childish, even, all sophistication washed away. The way she sometimes sounded late at night.

The funny thing, when she sat back she hardly said a word. She didn't act like she was angry or anything, she seemed cheerful enough, writing down some names on a scrap of paper. And the ride was over only a minute later, I could have been misreading her. The best way to say how she was, she'd hung up.

She was fine as we got out of the taxi, and, as I said, I could have misread her. But I went all hot and cold, I lost the feeling for being cool.

I didn't kiss her good night. I'd expected to right up until I saw she expected it too. I tried to play it that Vinnie Gold was a contrary bastard. "I had a nice time."

"Me too. Thanks, Vinnie."

She didn't look disappointed about the kiss.

# FORTY-TWO

I turned out the light. It was my way of reminding myself who was making this call. I liked being Vincenzo. I am Vincenzo, of course, but I felt like I was dressed up as a more confident form of myself in the dark. I could say anything. Be almost fearless. Almost.

I couldn't help the cold little zing that whizzed through my spine when I remembered how Vinnie's evening ended. Something had gone wrong, and I didn't know what it was. If I was ever going to turn this relationship into something more meaningful than a few phone calls, I was going to have to figure out how to do it. Soon.

"Hello, Quirino." Soft and blurry.

"Asleep?" I asked.

"Dozing."

"Dreaming?"

She giggled.

I asked, "Dreaming of me?" She sounded sweet as hell. She sounded better.

"If I dreamed of you, Questione, you'd be wearing a handkerchief. And you'd be taking me to the dance."

"I should have been expecting this, right?"

"I've been thinking about what you said," she told me. "That I don't see you as a person separate from these calls. In a way, you're right."

"The dance would change that?"

"I have a picture of you in my head, Quibble. You're perfect. Handsome, sensitive, sweet. Also sarcastic, smart-mouthed, challenging." A pause for effect. "If you don't tell me who you are soon, I'm not going to be able to reconcile reality with my ideal. You'll be a self-fulfilling prophecy."

"What we're talking about here are degrees of disappointment." I wanted to sound remote. Like this was a problem that didn't involve me personally. I don't think I made it.

"We're both going to want more." She sounded so cold. Really icy. "You because you'll think I know you as you are. But you can't possibly live up to the picture I'm creating."

"I told you before. I'm not somebody you'd date." I waited, but she didn't respond. "You're just beginning to realize it yourself."

"I didn't say that."

"Sure you did. You said I couldn't live up to your

imaginings," I said, treading water now and feeling some sand between my toes. "I knew that all along."

"That's not what I meant," she said.

"Ask your father," I said. "People are usually telling you the truth while they're saying something they didn't mean."

"Leave my father out of this."

"You said you weren't going to go anywhere with Biff again. That was a lie."

"No, it wasn't."

"I saw you come to school in his car after you said that."

"You don't understand. He'd have made a big scene."

"Did he ask you to the dance?"

"I told you, he isn't taking me. But I agreed to dance with him."

"He's sure to get the message if you keep saying yes."

Click.

I sighed, and dialed again.

She said, "Okay, maybe you're right. But I'll want to date someone sooner or later. I can't sit in the house on Saturday nights, Rocco."

I had the feeling I was being manipulated, and I hated it. Besides which, I had no intention of letting go of the bone when I had it so firmly in my teeth.

"Every time you get into his car, he's promising you he's trustworthy and you're promising him that you trust him. Soon you'll think you can't say no without hurting him deeply," I said. "Maybe that's true already. Meanwhile, he's telling everyone you're hot for him—"

"It doesn't matter."

"Because he's a football hero."

"No, Roberto, because other girls are hot for him and they won't believe I'm not. Anyway, before long he'll get interested in one of them and stop bothering me."

My anger dribbled away so fast, I had to catch it in a cup to have enough left to say, "Why do you need a boyfriend so badly, Patsy?"

"Unless you're interested in the position, don't go starting with the penny psychology."

"I just think you could make a better choice than an obscene caller, you know?"

"I don't think of you that way anymore," she wailed, frustrated.

"Maybe I should say something dirty."

"You can be so nice when you want to be, Rodolfo."

"Rodolfo? Where are you getting these?" As if I didn't know.

She said, "Listen, I'm asking you to go to the dance with me."

"What I said, some choice."

"I swear, I won't tell anyone about these calls."

"Me either."

"You still don't trust me," she said. "You don't trust. That's why you don't believe Biff could regret—"

I was laughing. "Did you hear yourself?"

"I don't have to like him to know there's a person in there. Maybe he's a person in pain. Did you ever—"

"You're calling him Biff, too. Ha-ha!"

Click.

I felt like an idiot. Vincenzo was an idiot. But what choice did I have?

I was afraid I'd do something to tip her off if I ever stepped out of the tight box that I'd built for Vinnie Gold. I'd messed up tonight, and I still didn't know what I'd done wrong. That's what I had to figure out.

As for Vincenzo, he had to remain closeted.

# FORTY-THREE

I left early the next morning. No school, so no need for the backpack. In fact, no one would have said a word to me if I'd stayed in bed. Strangely enough, I felt like getting up to run. I was eager to see what it was like to do it without the weight of books banging against my back.

The air was frigid when I went outside, the wind was brisk enough to make my eyes water, and there was no sun. Turned out it suited me. Last year I'd've been wrapped up like a snowman in this kind of weather. Here I was now, in only a sweat jacket, running down the street like a jock. It felt good.

I ran a few extra blocks in one direction, happy to be running and no one watching to see how I was doing. Then I heard a car several yards behind me. It stayed behind me.

When I turned to get a look at it, Mr. B was behind

the wheel. When he knew I'd seen him, he pulled up along-side me.

"Good boy. You're already up to a qualifying time."

I kept running and, taking the crest of a gently uphill slope, I raised a triumphant fist in the air. Mr. B got a charge out of that and returned the gesture as he drove on.

To tell you the truth, I got quite a charge out of it myself. I'd pared nearly two minutes off the previous morning's run. I felt great. What was racing speed, anyway? I'd ask Mr. B.

I spent the rest of the morning looking for another old essay and found one about learning to swim when you're afraid of the water. I don't know whether it was the early run or what, but I fell asleep as I lay on the bed, my pen scratch-ing over the notebook paper.

When I woke up, it was already getting dark. I looked around for something to eat, but Mom's cupboards were bare. No hidden brownies, no dry cereal to munch, no left-overs of any kind. But she'd probably do some shopping on the way home, I'd survive.

I checked the reading on the water in the aquarium and found it good. Dad wanted me to have it stabilized before we put any fish in there, but I wasn't sure how long he thought we'd have to wait. I called to ask, but no one was home at the other end.

I was in my room, rewriting the essay, when I heard Mom and Mr. B downstairs. Yelling. I opened the door to my room and listened from there. It wasn't necessary to go any far-ther. They were working their way in my direction.

"I can't believe you want to get into this now," Mom was saying.

"Get into what? I'm hungry, and I want to eat."

"I didn't do any shopping today. I didn't have time," Mom said. "We can go to that little restaurant on the boulevard."

"It's a diner," Mr. B said. "I don't like eating in diners."

"If you don't want to go out, we'll just order in."

"The boy has to be able to come home from school and find something besides eggs or tuna fish. There never seems to be anything else to eat. When he gets here, he has homework he needs to take care of, and he ought to be able to count on someone else having done the cooking."

I could get behind that.

My stomach growled.

"You're getting into dangerous territory there, Dom," Mom said, slipping into her feminist mode. Actually, I tended to agree with her—despite having taken a stand earlier—that I could do *some* of the cooking. So could Mr. B, and with my compliments, but I also agreed that Mom had to hold up her end.

"From now on," he said, "we go shopping together on the weekend, and we make sure we buy enough to get through a week and then some."

I headed downstairs to make sure they knew I was home. Just *seeing* me would probably calm things down. I went into the kitchen with a carefully bland expression in place. Just looking for snacks, that was my mission. It did create a lull in the, uh, conversation. Mom looked embarrassed, Mr. B still looked determined. Probably the man was just hungry.

"I'm not ordering in," Mr. B said. "I'll eat whatever's in the house tonight, but I'm not going out or ordering in."

Mom stood there and stared at Mr. B. I knew what was on her mind. She wanted him to say, "All right, let's go out, both of us being tired and hungry, and we'll work this out when we're feeling more relaxed." She wanted him to say, "I know this is working out differently than you thought it would, and I don't want you to be unhappy." Mom expected him to say that because it's the kind of thing Dad would have said.

12:00. Patsy picked up with, "Still mad at me?"

"I was mad?"

"You think I can't tell when you're mad?"

"Are you sure about who was mad last? I've lost track."

"Let's just have a serious conversation, okay?"

"We've had those."

"Don't try to sound like this has nothing to do with you. I tell you things I don't tell anyone else."

I knew right then where this was going. "You know my secrets too."

"It's not the same."

"No, and knowing who I am won't make it the same, either. It will just be different, and maybe not in such a good way."

Silence.

Finally she said, "I know it's hard to talk about feelings. Face to face, I mean. Especially for you, right?"

All right, I'll bite. "Why for me?"

"Isn't that the point of these calls?"

I didn't like her tone. And why was I the one with problems, anyway? I wasn't making a confidante of an obscene caller. "You mean we can talk because we're speaking anonymously?"

"You're speaking anonymously, Salvatore," she said. "You know who I am."

"Suppose you know me," I said. "Suppose I drop a card into your locker tomorrow. And then you find out who I am, who I really am. And you're sadly disappointed. How do you think we're both going to feel about that?"

"Suppose I find out who you are and I'm not disappointed in you. What then?"

"Not possible. Sometimes you're disappointed in me now."

"Okay, it's a point." I heard that little tapping thing going on. When she spoke again, it was with a fair amount of excitement in her voice. "You know, you've got something. But it's not that you're afraid you're— It's that you think you look good to me now, the you that I see every day at school—and that I'll know this dark and secret thing about you once I do know who you are. That's it. That's how you're afraid you'll be a disappointment."

Actually I didn't think that was it. Vinnie Gold already knew that wasn't it. I was willing to talk about it, though. "Okay, so let's say I'm out there, looking perfect to you. What then?"

"No one looks perfect to me, Sergio. Even perfect people have gaping holes in their underwear. The minute you get close to them, you get a glimpse of the underwear." She sighed, and added, "That would be just about everybody I know."

"All right," I said, a little breathlessly. "Hypothetically. You have this guy with holey underwear."

"Yeah?"

"What kind of guy is he?"

"Someone who won't say, I asked this girl out. Where does she get nerve to be sad or crabby, or maybe interested in anything besides me."

"What are you going to do for this hypothetical guy?"

"I . . . I guess I can accept him, just take him the way he is. It's what I'm asking for, isn't it?"

"Suppose you've already had that chance? Suppose you looked me over and found me wanting?"

"I'd say you never let me get to know you, not the way I know you now," she said. "Guys—no, not just guys," she corrected herself. "We all try to look just a little bit better than our real self. You only let me see you as you really are because we're on the phone, because I can't match your false face to your true identity."

"What if you're wrong?"

"Wrong, how?"

"Suppose this is my false face. What if I'm just talking a good game now, while you can't see me for who I really am—that loser who passes you in the hallway at school. Maybe being an obscene caller is the best I can aspire to."

"I guess you could have a mask for these talks," she said. "I hadn't thought of that, but I can handle it."

"Handle what?"

"That maybe it's not just that you're somebody I've always overlooked. Maybe you're somebody I wanted to overlook."

"So you can accept anything? Absolutely anything?"

"I think so," she said confidently. "I know the worst."

"What's the worst?"

"You make obscene phone calls." There was just the hint of a doubt in her voice now.

"There's something wrong here," I said. "You're assuming that because you know that, the rest of me can only be better."

"Isn't it?"

"I could be a cripple."

"I don't know anyone who's crippled, Sebastiano," she said, abandoning the philosophical approach.

"I could be excruciatingly poor, wearing hand-me-down jeans and never getting a decent haircut."

She made a sound under her breath, but she replied, "I don't know anyone like that, either."

"No one?"

"No." Trace of impatience.

"I think I might be disappointed in you."

She hung up.

Okay, so I was still mad.

# FORTY-FOUR

Taking my time, I ran four slow laps as Mr. B put the football team through a torturous session on some new equipment. Basically, the equipment looked like a section of a brick wall, and they rammed into it, leading with a shoulder. They looked surprisingly enthusiastic about the whole thing.

Thursday's day off stretched Biff's suspension through Friday. He watched the team take their punishment from a place high on the bleachers, clearly suffering from deprivation. I broke to do some stretching, silently congratulating myself for looking like a runner. For being one.

Biff stomped his way off the bleachers. He made the whole structure shake, and made a fair amount of noise too. I got the feeling he was admiring his style, much the way I'd been admiring mine.

No comparison, I said to myself with a little smile. That

was when I noticed Patsy. She was standing just inside the school doors, staring out at me. Or Biff.

I left the track, heading her way. My feelings about her were mixed—confused, even—but I'd be cool. I raised a hand only moments ahead of the football team's arrival at the same spot, a herd of great cattle, manageable only when forced into single file. They swept me past her by about ten feet, I don't know how I avoided being trampled. I didn't know how she did.

If she did. When I looked back, she'd gone.

She could go three ways from there, including up to the next floor. I decided to let her go for the moment. I got to my locker about thirty seconds ahead of Biff, who was half a dozen lockers away.

He passed me, making quite a point of ignoring me. I mean, if he'd just gone about his business and all, he would've been ignoring me. But he made a point of it. Stashing his stuff in his locker. Hopping around, doing warm-ups. Sighing and grunting like he was exerting himself tremendously. Letting me know he'd completely forgotten I was there.

Not that anybody was as aware of him as I was. There were guys yodeling into their lockers and snapping towels at each other. There was the usual foot traffic to and from the showers, a lot of horsing around. Biff was all but invisible to nearly everyone.

I stretched—long, simple stretches that were almost a meditation. I changed clothes slowly. Cold-syrup slow. I made it a test of endurance to move so slowly, even my breathing was slow. Finally he shut his locker and headed off for a class.

I wasn't far behind, making it to my class as the bell rang.

The funny thing, the slowness stayed with me. I was slow with a slothlike gracefulness that I associated with dancing.

The girls had gotten this idea to wear pink or red for Valentine's Day. Most of them were carrying heart-shaped boxes of candy, some of them carried more than one.

Twice I saw guys slipping envelopes through the slots in a locker, and there was such a frenzy of card-giving that I got a couple. Nothing serious, kind of joke cards. It was fun, really, and now and then I felt a wistful twinge. I wished I'd brought a card for Patsy.

Daniel nodded when I sat down at the table in the cafeteria. I nodded back. "You join the track team?" he asked me.

"I'm going to try for it."

"I run on Forest Avenue most mornings. We could run together."

I asked him, "You're on the track team?"

He grinned. "I'm going to try for it."

I hesitated, then said, "I've seen you talking to Patsy."

"I know Patsy pretty well," he said, blushing. "She has this friend, Melanie—"

"Melanie's cute," I said. "Forest Ave., huh?"

* * *

I stayed after school to give Mr. B a hand with three filing cabinets he wanted to move out of his office. He helped me get his oversized desk out of the way. Because he'd had the football team slamming into their fake walls that afternoon, I ended up moving the cabinets myself.

I shifted half the contents of each file drawer to a cardboard box, carrying the box and then the half-emptied drawer to a bench in the locker room. Then shoved the considerably lighter filing cabinet through the locker room to a closet. Finally I put the drawers back and stuffed the rest of the files back in. First cabinet down.

The files were pretty interesting. Brown Bunny's hoody guy? Likely to be another Albert Einstein. He's not in advanced classes because he won't do homework. Not that I could just settle in and read, but the occasional glance at what I was moving made for some lively thought.

After an hour of shifting and lugging and sliding, I was tired. It was a helluva time for Biff to come along. "Hey, turd."

I stopped pushing the last filing cabinet and leaned wearily against it. I had the feeling he'd said something to me once already, something I hardly heard over the scrape of metal against the floor. The shifty look in his eyes made me suspect that he'd turned to look over his shoulder before he called out again. No one else was around.

"You think you got nothing to worry about, huh? Cozying

up to your stepdaddy?" He closed the distance between us. "Moving his shit around."

I didn't open my mouth. But I was thinking, practice must be about to end. This hallway would be full of life in a minute or two.

"You think somebody's gonna come along and save your ass? Forget it, they're all still on the field. You better say something, turd."

The first real blow came fast, so that I didn't have a chance to be ready for it. It caught me just under the ribs, solid enough to fold me over. It's always surprising when someone with Biff's bulk moves quickly.

The next one was where you'd expect, but he didn't put any weight behind it. It was practically like he chucked me under the chin, but it brought me back up enough to face him.

I tasted blood.

"Ah, ah, ah," he said to himself. For my benefit, he added, "We don't want to leave any marks, do we?"

I gathered he'd learned something from suspension.

He landed one in my chest, good enough to slam me into the corner of a filing cabinet, which caught me under the shoulder blade. I shifted away, into a row of lockers, re-visited by the wave of self-loathing I'd felt after the mugging. I'd hoped never to feel that kind of disgust again, at least not for myself. I tried to recall some of the moves I'd learned from those self-defense books.

Frankly, I had abandoned the books once I figured out

they didn't offer much in the way of an immediate solution. Now I had the expectation of violence, and none of the moves.

The other picture that came to mind, Patsy standing outside my door, waiting to hear why I fought with him the first time. If I hated myself now, how was I going to feel when I had to face her again? As if the thought had sprung into my eyes, Biff addressed that very subject.

"You shouldn't get any ideas, living next door to my girl the way you do. You shouldn't think she'll fall for your smarts."

It really hadn't occurred to me that she liked to see evidence of intelligence. I mean, what other choice of boyfriend had I seen her make? But clearly, Biff felt threatened.

"I don't believe she is your girlfriend."

"You won't hold her attention for long, Gold, but I don't want you distracting her."

I felt the first flare of real anger, going off like fireworks. It felt good. Hot, colorful, good. He hit me in the shoulder, slamming me into the lockers.

"You know what I think?" he said, pushing his face into mine.

"Give me a minute. I'll get it," I said conversationally. This was not courage speaking, not even false bravado. This was suicidal. "I doubt that you do enough of it to come up with anything terribly original."

A quick one, two, three to the ribs, leaving me nearly breathless.

"We're gonna do this often, Gold, have these little talks, you and me, anytime I think you need reminding. There's a scientific word for that, right, Gold? I hear you're real sharp in science."

A sense of utter futility washed through me, leaving me weak and nauseated.

"What's the word, Gold?" he asked, and I sensed it was a rhetorical question, because he landed another in my gut. I was looking at the floor again.

The double doors swung open as some guys charged in, coming from outside. I was aware of the doors, of cold air, of the charge coming to a sudden halt.

"The word, smart-ass," Biff said, tapping me on the shoulder hard enough I almost fell to my knees. "What's it called, you learning not to do something I don't like?"

The one and only thing those self-defense books ever impressed upon me was how much power a fist could pack, not just a fist shoved straight out but one that is turning from a thumb-up position to a thumb-down position while it's shooting forward. Something about that twisting motion increases the punch. That's the kind of shot I directed at Biff as I came out of that crouched position. He wasn't expecting it. And it landed lucky, not on the chin the way I planned but under it, fitting into the angle where chin meets throat.

The effect it had on Biff was astounding. He squawked, choked, and struggled to breathe, tears suddenly streaming down his face, and as he choked, he backed into the bench that ran along the row of lockers, tripping backward over it with another weird squeal, continuing his fight for air, heels up.

I watched all this, not quite believing my eyes and making no effort to help him. I don't think I could have helped if I had known what to do. I was entirely without emotion. And after a few seconds, he began to recover, which is to say, he started to breathe. Not easily, and not with complete satisfaction, but well enough that I was sure he would live.

I slid my foot a little way under the bench and tapped his leg with the toe of my shoe. "'Behavior modification' is the word you're looking for," I said.

I saw Mr. B sitting in his office as I went back for the last filing cabinet. I knew he'd been keeping an eye on me, and he'd probably followed Biff back in, entering his office from the hallway rather than the locker room. That he knew Biff and I had had a small altercation. That he hadn't interfered—not when it looked like I might die, not when it looked like Biff might die.

He waved me into his office.

"I had to make a stand," I said. I was testing my voice, my footing, testing reality. Found I was dry as a bone.

"You made a good one," Mr. B said. "I knew you would. Better get some ice for that lip. Let me drive you home tonight."

# FORTY-FIVE

First stop, the drugstore. "Just want to pick up a card for your mother," Mr. B said. He also went to the supermarket next door and got her some roses, leaving me to think about whether I could still get Patsy a card. Slip it under her door.

It felt too risky, that's what I kept coming back to. I regretted that I hadn't given her a card at school. But now? What if she saw me cross the driveway? Even if she didn't, it would be like drawing a dotted line with a big arrow pointing to me.

Mr. B surprised me when he stopped again to pick up three take-out meals from a place that advertised itself as a family restaurant. They looked happy to see him, called him Dom.

"This is where I ate while I waited for you and your mother to move out here," he explained.

"Smells good."

"Great meatballs," he said. "You like spaghetti and meatballs? You could live on these meatballs alone."

I had been thinking along other lines. First manicotti, now this. "You aren't worried Mom will think you're backing down on the home-cooked-meal stance? I mean, I'm all for what works—"

I just wasn't looking forward to another argument.

"First, no. Your mom needs a little more help from me, is all. Maybe I should have known that would be true, all that time she spends on the train. And second, we don't build relationships like we make a business deal. It's give-and-take, and a lot of the time it doesn't work out to be fifty-fifty. It's always shifting."

I didn't have to come up with a reply, because the waiter came over to take our orders. "Three number fours," Mr. B said. "And an extra side of meatballs."

In the car, I put my face into the bag and breathed deeply of dinner. As if it was nothing to do with nothing, Mr. B said, "You shouldn't worry about your mother and me. We're going to do fine." I was glad to hear he felt that way. I went on breathing meatballs.

Mom was in the dining room when Mr. B and I got home, standing on a chair to hang something up on the wall, and without looking in our direction she told me to hand her the thumbtacks.

"This worked for us once," she said, "and it'll work for us

again." I saw that Mom had made yet another chart assigning chores, but the division of labor was better proportioned. Plus, if my olfactory senses could be relied on, she had a chicken in the oven.

"What happened to you?" she asked as she stepped off the kitchen chair. It was hide-your-horror, toned down about fifty percent.

"Nothing, really nothing," I said, feeling, sad to say, a certain pride.

"He's okay," Mr. B said, from behind me. Had stopped to check the oven. "A drawer opened while he was moving the filing cabinet for me."

"I've decided I like the bruised-and-battered look," I said, to discourage Mom from looking too closely at this story. "I'm going to start talking like Marlon Brando. It's bound to attract girls, don't you think?"

"Is this your blood?" Mom had found a telltale blot on my shirt.

"Would it be better if it belonged to somebody else?" I asked her, and she laughed.

I felt fine, even better, knowing Mr. B had not started a phone chain—calling Mom, who would then call Dad—the minute I was out of sight.

Mr. B said, "Don't start with the doctor business again."

Mom said, "But there's swelling, Dom."

"Sure there is. That drawer clobbered him." He looked in the oven again, and I caught a glimpse of foil-wrapped lumps.

"Stop opening the oven door." Mom pointed to the table, at the salad. And a container of sour cream.

Actually, Mr. B looked like he'd died and gone to heaven. Roast chicken! Baked potatoes! And sour cream! Salad—well, yeah, salad. Ya gotta take the bad with the good.

"What's that in the bags?" Mom asked.

"Sunday dinner," Mr. B said. "It'll reheat."

Over the chicken, Mom made one more foray into overanxious-mother territory. "I think the swelling is worse. Dom, does he look worse to you?"

I reached for a second helping.

Mr. B looked at the chicken, making sure he'd find a third helping on the platter. "It'll be better in the morning," he said.

Probably because I looked unconcerned, Mom said, "You look like a raccoon with an underbite."

"Don't say that. I'm going to the dance tomorrow night, and I don't want to look like I think the holiday is Halloween."

"Taking that girl next door?" Mr. B asked.

"I'm going alone," I said, "and I think she is too." A silence followed. I couldn't leave it at that. "It's a little early in our relationship to go to a dance as a couple."

Mom had a little announcement of her own. "I'm going back to work full-time next week. I'm not doing enough with the day or two I have free. And with some of the extra money, I can have somebody come in and clean once a week. Is that okay with you, Dom?"

"Sure," he said with a shrug. "I was thinking about that.

For the housekeeping, I mean. Are you sure you want to work more hours?"

"To tell you the truth, I get a little bored with too many days off."

Mom seemed to think she'd come to a momentous decision, and maybe it was. There was a part of me that wished she'd made this discovery sooner, with less upheaval.

But there was a bigger part of me that had already accepted that things had changed, and the changes were irreversible. I hoped they were going to be good changes in the long run. We'd just have to wait and see.

Mr. B helped clear the table. Mom said she would throw a coffee cake together so they'd have something to munch in front of the TV. She was talking about a boxed mix, of course, but Mr. B didn't have a thing against it.

I went through a couple of boxes in my closet to find a Fonz mask Dad had picked up for two bucks in a costume shop a year or so ago. Marred only by a couple of hairline cracks, it was made from a super-flexible rubber with a thin cotton lining. It folded into a small bundle that I could stuff into my gym locker Saturday morning.

I decided to pull a bulky turtleneck sweater over my silk shirt to disguise it. The sweater wasn't much, but if things went the way I hoped, we'd be in the dark, and the rough wool was a far cry from my actual costume.

* * *

"Tomasino."

"I'll meet you at the dance," I said, wanting to get it out before my courage died. Good thing, because I regretted it even as the words were coming out of my mouth.

"What kind of mask will you be wearing?"

"Maybe you want me to wear a sign."

"How will we meet, then?"

I was shaking all over. "There's a room on the second floor. Right above the principal's office."

"I know where you mean. Textbooks go in there during the summer."

I guess that explained all the empty metal shelving. I only knew the health-class movies Mr. B showed were stored in there. I said, "It won't be locked."

"That's where we'll meet?" Now she sounded a little shaky.

"Inside."

"I don't know."

"At ten after nine, you go in. Alone. I'll follow you in at twelve after."

"How will I know it's you?"

"Who else would be there?"

"Are we going to turn on the lights?" she asked.

"Hanging around with Biff is getting on your nerves."

"Stop it. I just need to think this over."

"Tomorrow night. Ten after nine. Okay?"

I halfway thought she wouldn't go for it. A part of me was already feeling resigned, a satellite after all.

"You couldn't just ask me to dance?"

"You're kidding, right?"

"You'll be nice to me, won't you?"

"We won't discuss Biff at all."

She sighed. "See you there."

Click.

Once I'd hung up, I found myself too nervous to sleep. To stay in bed. Patsy's room was dark, I saw when I looked out the window. But then, so was mine, and I pulled back quickly.

I imagined opening the door to the book room and finding half my class there, waiting to see an obscene caller. Maybe I should prepare a short speech. Maybe the principal would be standing there, clued in by an anonymous phone call made in a sweet, clear voice. Maybe she'd have the cops there and she would say, *That's him, he's the one*.

Stranger things had happened.

I dialed again, standing just shy of the window.

"Umberto?"

"I'm happy to say I'm not afflicted with it," I said. Then added, "I just want you to know, you're safe with me."

"You called back to tell me that?" she asked in a voice that smiled. "You really are nice."

"That's what you said about Biff."

"Not really," she said.

If I'd even breathed, I'd never have heard her hang up.

A wave of nausea washed over me, knocking me back to the sandy beach of my bed. I didn't try to get up again. Better to lie there with the water lapping at my sides.

# FORTY-SIX

I told Mr. B I was going running, but I had bigger things to do, too. He had Saturday-morning practice, and we ate breakfast together.

"You know your mom and I will be out late tonight?"

"She told me."

"Don't forget your house keys," he said. "And have a good time at the dance."

Outside, Dad was parked at the curb. He got out of the taxi as I walked down the driveway.

"Hey, Dad, is something wrong?"

"Everything's fine, Vinnie. Nothing to worry about." I was already realizing that was true. He looked . . . happy. He held out a gallon-sized water-filled plastic bag. "I brought you a couple of fish. Canaries to your coal mine."

"I think the chemistry is good," I said. There were two

angelfish trying to maintain some stability in the quivering bag. "They're beautiful."

"Go drop the bag in the tank. Their water temp has to adjust before you open the bag."

"I remember." I tossed my backpack into the car.

Dad took a closer look at me. "You got into another fight?"

I pulled one shoulder up in half a shrug. "I was moving a filing cabinet and the drawer slid out."

"Nothing's broken?"

"It doesn't look that bad, does it?"

"Swellings are worse in the morning. I think. Same drawer that hit you before?"

"Not a word to Mom. Mr. B covered for me."

This wasn't quite enough to relieve Dad's mind. "Is it over with now?"

"I think so. I hit him back this time. Big surprise to both of us. Why are you here so early? You don't usually drive at this hour, do you?"

"I took a different shift. I've got a small part in a film. Three lines."

"Cool."

Mr. B was coming out as I took the fish in, on his way to a practice. He saw Dad, said good morning, and shook hands. From the bay window, I saw there was a little eyebrow action from Dad, probably questioning whether the trouble with Biff was really over, and Mr. B made a little punching motion and clapped him on the shoulder.

"They look like they might get along," Mom said as she came up behind me. I agreed, although I didn't care to get all aren't-we-all-one-big-happy-family about it.

"Do me a favor? Open the bag and let them out in an hour or so, okay?"

"Sure."

When I got back outside, Mr. B and Dad were laughing together, and then Mr. B was on his way. It was sort of a relief that he was. It was fine with me that Dad and Mr. B didn't have to be enemies, but I wasn't ready to stand around being the son and the stepson at the same time. Not yet.

Dad saw me coming and said, "I've been wanting to talk to you, son. How's about I join you for a turn around the track?"

He drove me to the school, not talking much. When we got out, we avoided looking in the direction of Mr. B and the team. We walked around the track, partly because Dad hasn't been becoming a runner, but more because I didn't feel we were doing this so I could show my stuff. About the second time around, Dad got up his nerve.

"I don't know how you're going to take this, Vinnie. But I'm seeing someone."

"You're entitled. You don't have to get my okay."

"I felt like I needed to."

"You don't need to. Do I know her?"

"It's Mona."

"Mona the meddler?" I asked, to seem surprised.

"She's a nice woman."

"She is! I like her. I feel like we've always known her, right?"

"Lately she started bringing over these posters to put on the wall," Dad said. "I asked her to hang around, have a bite to eat. We got to know each other without all the noise."

"Other people looking on."

"I know this is hard on you. But I can't wait until you're too old to care what I'm doing with my life," he said, with just a trace of impatience.

I said, "I'm glad you're happier."

"I'm glad your mother's happier," Dad said. "Frankly, I think I'm happier. I want what's best for all of us, and it may turn out, someday, that right now we're in the painful process of getting just that."

That hung in the air between us for what seemed like a long time. And I can't say it didn't get to me. I finally formed a response to it. "I hope you know, I won't be feeling sorry for you anymore."

Dad laughed and said, "God, that'll be a relief."

I expected to find the locker room empty.

"Hey, Gold, you joining the track team?"

This from a wiry senior. He was already on the team, and even though the dean had introduced me to him, I was uncertain how good a reception I was going to get.

"Better the track team than the buffalo boys," I said, hoping he didn't have a wider brother on the football team.

"Good thinking," he said. "My brother's going to be the

time to beat. Dancing made him strong. Fast. Not all those ballerinas are lightweights, you know."

"Daniel," I said, grinning.

"Yeah." Some kind of big-brother protectiveness came into play. "You don't think ballet is sissy, do you?"

I laughed. "I won a quickstep competition a couple of years ago."

"Quickstep?"

"Ballroom dancing. I hope there's room for more than one of us on the team."

"Oh, yeah, but he's going to be the star."

"We'll see." I slipped the bundled-up mask out of my backpack and into my gym locker. It started to unroll, but I yanked the sweater out of my backpack and covered it up. I left both items in the locker.

When I was thirteen and fourteen, I went out trick-or-treating with a black satin cape Dad got from a bit part he did in a movie. I didn't go so much for the candy as for the excuse to swoop around in a cape that made me feel a little wild. Bold.

Juvenile stuff, I know, but between you and me, I keep that cape hanging in my closet. Sometimes I even put it on when I'm just in my room or something. Probably a touch of theatrical blood in my veins.

That night, I pulled out those black leather pants that happened to be terrific now that seriously cold weather had set in, and matched them with a black silk shirt I wore for dance contests. The cape no longer brushed against my heels like the first time I'd worn it, but it hung below my knees. Good enough.

I stood close to the mirror and slowly turned my face from side to side. Not too bad. A faint discoloration. The fat lip was only a little pouty. I cut eye holes in a strip of black T-shirt fabric and tied it over my face like a headband. I was slick. Symbolic.

Zorro.

I cut a few moves in front of the mirror. More than were strictly necessary to know if the cape worked, which it did— it shimmied, it swirled, it draped, like great hair.

And then I headed out.

Mr. B's school keys were on his dresser. Although I would no doubt get home before he and Mom did, I just slipped the marked book room key off the ring, leaving the key ring lying there where he'd left it. I thought it over and removed the bar dogger that would open the gates that stretched across the ends of the corridors after hours. He wouldn't miss the keys even if I had to wait until tomorrow to return them. Mr. B wouldn't bother with anything but his car keys until Monday. The man was regular as a prison guard.

# FORTY-SEVEN

I left my coat in my gym locker. It covered the mask and sweater, still hidden inside. I put on the cape, tied on the strip of black mask. I got a few glances in the locker room, but no comments. There were a lot of white suits vying for the *Saturday Night Fever* look; there was a Lawrence of Arabia and a cowboy.

"Butch Cassidy?" I asked the cowboy.

"Sundance Kid," he said. "That's who got the girl."

I nodded.

"Zorro?" he hesitated a moment. "I don't remember him getting the girl."

"Maybe not on TV," I said. "In the movies, he did."

"Cool."

The gym had been transformed. Everyone entered

through double doors that had been framed with a big heart shape outfitted with red and pink balloons.

Inside, disco lights flashed to the Bee Gees' beat. There were balloons clinging to the ceiling and long streamers dangling, some with glittering paper hearts that reflected the lights, others with red glass beads sparkling.

Garlands were strung around the room to draw the eye to posters of famous movie romances. *Gone with the Wind*, *Love Story*, *Annie Hall*, and *West Side Story* were the ones that caught my eye. And the DJ was dressed in a white suit, his dark hair shiny and styled like Travolta's.

The floor was already filled with dancers.

I didn't see Patsy.

I made the rounds of the room, checking out the dance floor. Most of the girls wore sequined cat's-eye masks, but they were costumed in everything from frilly period gowns to slinky black dresses.

The guys wore black eye masks or strips of black silk tied Zorro-style, like my own. With most of them, their pants and shirts were, on the whole, harder to figure. Open collars and rolled-up cuffs could have meant anyone from Humphrey Bogart to Ryan O'Neal. Some tried for more romantic silhouettes, wearing loose-sleeved shirts and tied-back hair. There were a surprising number of guys with capes, long and short.

Biff walked in. He was not wearing Patsy on his arm. No mask, either. A sheepish look seemed to be all the costume he believed he needed.

I'd just finished paying for a soda when Patsy came in with somebody I didn't recognize. She was a surprise. Her hair was pulled up into ponytails over each ear. She wore Bermuda shorts and a little top. Her arms were bare. Alabaster and bare. I just love girls' arms, so thin and straight.

She turned to her friend, the boy next door to her Gidget, and grinned. He loped off, making a beeline for a girl wearing white tennis shoes and a wide pink skirt with a black poodle appliqué. I took a step in Patsy's direction, but Brown Bunny got there first, with a couple of other girls in tow.

So I made it my business to circulate, stopping to say hi to several people I recognized and to compliment a caped highwayman on his costume. Daniel nodded to me as he walked Melanie to the dance floor. I crossed paths with Biff on my rounds. We didn't speak, and he didn't pretend not to see me. We more or less pretended not to know each other.

I lounged around with my soda in hand while Patsy danced a few, including one dance with Biff. She didn't make a point of snubbing him, anyway. He didn't hold her hand on the way to the floor. He didn't look at her once they were dancing—he simply leaned from side to side like a wind-tossed palm tree—instead, he was looking around the gym, making sure everyone saw him with her. Sort of Biff enjoying being Biff. He made no connection with Patsy.

As for Patsy, her heart wasn't in it. I thought she definitely had her eye on me. Whenever I let my eyes drift in her direction, she looked away from my general vicinity.

Biff stopped swaying long before "I Heard It Through the Grapevine" finished, said something to her, and left her standing on the floor. Patsy drifted in my direction. She stopped only a couple of steps away, and asked, "Errol Flynn?"

I shook my head. "Tyrone Power."

I tried to think of something to follow this up. Zorro had gone all strong and silent on me. Patsy kept her eyes carefully trained on the dance floor.

She asked, "Did you come with anybody?"

"I didn't know if I'd come. I don't really have a group to hang around with. So I didn't ask anybody."

This got a nod.

I noticed her socks. They were these cute girl socks—the ankle section was a dog's body; the folded-over part was a puppy's face with a tongue hanging out. I wanted to laugh, but it felt wrong at just that moment.

I said, "Dance?"

"Sure, I'd like to," she said.

I stepped away to get rid of the untouched soda, my chest tight with anticipating the dance, the girl. I had hopes of getting something faster to dance to, something to burn off my nervous energy.

She waited indifferently as I came back to her, now hardly acknowledging my invitation to dance. But this didn't bother me—I had a feeling I knew this side of her from talking to her late at night, the hope that she wouldn't seem too clueless, or in this case, too eager.

I took her hand and led her to the edge of the dancers. I

got lucky. An Eagles song, "Take It to the Limit." Hardly anybody but a dancer knows that's a waltz. I drew Patsy up against me like I didn't think she could find her way, leading in true ballroom fashion. She looked at me in surprise.

Her hand slipped beneath the cape up to my shoulder, I could feel the skin of her bare arm right through the silk shirt. I felt my belly tighten but let a smile play across my lips as I drew back to look at her. I saw the curiosity in Patsy's eyes, highlighted by a twinge of apprehension.

I swear I could feel her heart beating as I whirled her onto the dance floor. She stayed right with me. I felt something—some pressure in my chest—let go all at once. Easing back. I was happy, the way dancing always made me happy. Patsy looked confident, and for a good reason—Patsy could dance.

The magic came.

Next, we drew "Devil with a Blue Dress." I released her and started to move to the beat. She did too, and she was sassy, sexy. Fun. The waltz had warmed us up, left us with a calm, focused energy, a boost of creativity. When I moved in closer, she matched her moves to mine, as if she'd found a pattern in them, and she began to anticipate them with complementary moves of her own. We danced within inches of each other.

A group of observers formed a roomy circle around us, but we hardly noticed except to make use of the extra floor space as we segued into the next piece of music, Grace Jones singing—no question of whether we'd stop dancing. The magic held. We were enjoying ourselves. We were having fun.

On the last notes, I spun away from Patsy. Corny, but effective. A few kids actually clapped, the disjointed applause made us aware that we were still being watched. Made me aware of ol' Biff standing there with two sodas in his hands.

Patsy and I stared at each other over a distance of about six feet. I was giving her a chance to walk away. She didn't. The music started again, something slower. I swooped in and dipped her, let the cape drape over us. Our faces were only a few inches apart.

I held on to Patsy and led again. When Mom insisted I take dancing lessons with Dad and her, she said all the guys she'd ever slow-danced with were fumblers at worst and just adequate at best. Patsy was cool. Not too cool. Her heart was going at a pretty good clip. We were close, and we were wearing clothing thin enough to appreciate it.

I shifted into a more complex step, punctuated with turns and stops. She was with me all the way. The cape swept around her at every turn, holding her enclosed with me for a moment before we moved again, whispering over the bare skin of her arm as it fell back again. I never took my eyes off her face, although much of the intensity on both of our faces must have had to do with the effort we put into dancing. The music ended.

Patsy didn't pull away. I spotted the clock over the double doors. Ten minutes to nine. I said, "Your boyfriend has your soda." I let go of her and turned with a swish of cape before she could put on a polite face. It was worth the whole evening, the whole everything, to see that look in her eyes. She wanted to go on dancing. With me.

# FORTY-EIGHT

It was hard to go. I felt like I was breaking a connection, like I was hanging up. But I continued out of the gym and headed for the boys' locker room like I was going to the john. I went straight to my locker and grabbed the sweater with the mask balled up inside it. I fished in my pocket for the bar dogger to open the hallway. I raced up the stairs.

The upstairs hallway was dim as I opened the metal gate, gratefully acknowledging the inspiration that made me take the dogger. I pulled the gate closed behind me and raced to the other end to open the one Patsy would need to pass through.

Then back to the appointed meeting place. This door didn't have a window like the classroom doors. And I'd stood on the table to loosen the lightbulb yesterday afternoon. There'd be no light in the room once the door was closed. I had trouble with the key. The lock was a little tight. I could swear I heard the scrape of shoes on the stairs. Shoes that were trying not to make too much noise.

Finally the bolt shifted. I opened the door, flicked the light switch a couple of times to be sure no one had screwed the bulb back in, then dashed down the hall to the john. I glanced at the hall clock. Ten after. I slipped inside and stood still, listening.

Not a sound.

I closed the door silently. She would come. She had to. I tore off the cape and pulled the turtleneck over my shirt. Took off Zorro's eye mask and stood behind the door of the john, peeping out.

Where was she?

I was just about to open the door to listen again when I saw her. Timid. Looking up and down the hallway before she tried the door, pushed it open while standing as far away from it as she could. I could just hear her voice, presumably calling out an Italian name. I grinned as I pulled the mask over my face.

I didn't move until she went in, then I tiptoed across the hall and stood there for a moment, trying to breathe normally. No good. I could stand there until midnight, but I wasn't going to feel normal in any way. The rubbery smell of the mask made me feel faint.

I opened the door as narrowly as possible, slipped inside, and shut it quickly behind me, hoping the light from the hallway hadn't allowed her to identify me by my shoes or the way I moved. At least, by arriving last and leaving first, I had some control over how long she could see me at all.

Patsy reached out and touched my arm. "I thought you'd get here sooner," I said, deepening my voice.

"I couldn't get away from my friends. They were all excited about something that happened downstairs." She didn't take her hand away. I was glad. It was so dark in the room that it was like talking through a tunnel. It was like talking on the phone.

"I like your socks."

"Not exactly glamorous."

"I admit it. I was way off base." I knew she'd like hearing that.

"You still sound like you're talking through a handkerchief."

"It's the mask."

"I saw it when you came in," Patsy said. "It's dark in here now."

"Pitch-black," I agreed. I reached for her hand, still resting on my arm, and felt my way to the table I knew was in the center of the room. All of about three feet. I pulled off the mask and took a breath of fresh air, setting the mask down.

Patsy's voice had gone high and childlike. "Now that we're here, I don't know what to say."

I didn't answer, but found her other hand in the darkness. I was not feeling suave. I let my fingers drift up her arms, then her neck. Her skin was incredible. My hands

249

were shaking. She couldn't have taken it for anything but fear. I touched the little ponytails. Silky blond hair between my fingers.

The shaking had spread all through me. Even my breathing shook as I leaned toward her. Maybe some of it was Patsy. I hoped so. Her lips were soft against mine. Eventually the space between our bodies closed. It was a while before we came up for air. When we did, we leaned against each other and I took in the scent of her hair.

"Are you going to tell me who you are?" she whispered.

I shook my head, loving the way her hair felt against my face. "Not yet."

"Are you going to call tonight?"

"Twelve o'clock on the dot."

She sighed.

I let my face slip over hers, exploring the contours with my own cheek and with my lips. We kissed again—my mouth was open, and after a moment hers opened beneath mine. When our tongues touched, it startled us both and we drew back slightly, our lower lips barely touching. The heat that had built up between us was astounding.

"Patsy." It killed me to do it, but I pulled away. "I'm going to go back downstairs."

"No."

"We have to," I said. "I'll go first."

I grabbed my mask and pulled it on.

"Wait," she said.

I turned back and, lifting the mask, gave her a quick

peck on the cheek. "You wait," I whispered. "Give me a minute."

"Won't you tell me who you are?"

"Soon." I slipped through the door, shutting it behind me, and dashed for the john. Stripping off my current disguise, I listened for her to shut the book room door. By that time I was Zorro again.

I dropped the Fonz mask and the sweater out the window. I flipped the lights off in the hallway and ran, yanking the gate shut. I wanted to beat her back to the gym. I flashed through the locker room, stopping only to check that my eye mask looked undisturbed.

I strolled out of the locker room and back into the gym, heading for the back wall. Patsy came through the double doors only a moment later, followed by three girls. They were all aflutter about something. I wondered whether Patsy had said anything to them about our meeting.

Biff walked over to her with an ugly expression. I stepped into the soda line. Her girlfriends stood by her, flapping their hands at him, shooing him away. A teacher came over and sent him on his way.

Patsy danced a couple of times with some other guys. She was more than lively. She was agitated.

I didn't ask her to dance. I was still shaking. And to tell you the truth, I could still feel the length of her against me. I couldn't have danced with her again without communicating some of that to her.

I was bothered by the answer I'd tossed over my shoulder,

"soon." Did I mean it? If I didn't mean it, she was not going to take it well. I hadn't really thought things through. I should never have arranged to meet her. Or at least I should never have shown up.

I was an idiot.

Apparently, I was not the only one. Whatever Biff's problem was, and it must have been her thirty-minute disappearance, he wouldn't let it go. He cut in on a dance and Patsy stayed on the floor, but they didn't look like they were enjoying each other's company.

# FORTY-NINE

I'd planned to jog home.

I wanted to pick up the sweater and the mask first. I was on my way through the parking lot to get them when I saw Patsy and Biff, a cloud of heated breath fogging the air between them. She threw her arms in the air in a dismissive gesture and started to walk away. He went after her and grabbed her arm. Another burly type stepped in to tell Biff to lay off. By then I was close enough to hear what was being said.

"I don't have to go home with you," she said angrily. "I can walk." What struck me, she was wearing sweatpants for warmth, very un-Patsy. The ponytails jiggled merrily with every move she made.

"All I said was, you're not acting right."

"Better, then, that you don't have to put up with me."

"Patsy," Daniel put in. "You can ride with me and Melanie. It's too late to walk."

Then Patsy saw me. "I can walk with Vinnie. He lives right next door to me. Okay, Vinnie?"

"Sure. Okay."

Melanie viewed the situation with obvious approval. I think I already knew she wasn't exactly a member of Biff's fan club. Patsy and I said good night. Biff stood there until we were maybe thirty feet away. Then he got into his car with a heavy slam of the door and drove off.

"Thanks, Vinnie," Patsy said. Nothing pathetic or even particularly humble. Like we were friends and friends do this sort of thing for each other.

"Sure."

"You're a terrific dancer."

I shrugged that off.

"My dad taught ballroom at Arthur Murray while he was putting himself through school," she said.

I grinned. "That's where I learned."

"You could've asked me to the dance."

I shook my head. "I really wasn't sure I'd go."

"Are girls here so unsophisticated, compared to the ones you know in New York?"

I raised my eyebrows. "We're still in New York."

"This is the Island," she said derisively, and as she went on, she was imitating Brown Bunny. "'There's all of Queens between here and New York.' Queens with three *e*'s," she told me with a grin.

"She's from Manhattan?" I leapt at the first opportunity to steer the conversation in another direction. Toward Brown Bunny, toward anyone else. "Your friend, I mean."

"Does that make her more interesting?"

"Not as a date. You ask a lot of questions," I said, trying for polite exasperation. It always works in the movies.

"At first I thought you were shy. Now I get the feeling you're trying to be the strong, silent type," she said, undaunted. "Has somebody in your past made that seem desirable? Or are you shy?"

"That's two."

She laughed.

I started to laugh, too, but I choked it back. Laughter is like a fingerprint. The sound that came out was something of a snort, like I was making fun of the reason for her laughter. There was nothing I could do about it.

She sighed, then muttered, "I'm sorry." She looked like she'd had a tough evening. "I didn't mean to sound like my dad. And I didn't mean to get you involved back there. You've had your share of run-ins with him."

I wanted to reach out to touch her arm, to comfort her. But that would be out of character. I could say something like . . . oh, I don't even know, but something that would come off the way I danced with her.

But since then, I'd held her in the darkness. The thought of reaching for her now made me start to shake again. I hoped it would pass for the shivers. We didn't talk, walking fast because it really was cold.

After a while I became aware of a tiny sound she seemed to be trying not to make, and it sounded suspiciously sniffly. At first I thought she just had a runny nose, it was cold out. Her face was turned slightly away, so I moved in close enough to lean around her as we walked.

A wet trail down her cheek reflected the light from a streetlamp, and when she stopped, I wiped it away with my thumb. Yes, shaking. "I don't usually have this effect on girls," I said.

She laughed in a sloppy kind of way, spraying tears on my hand. Standing in the glow of the streetlight, I put my arm around her shoulders and held on, feeling sort of stoic. It was easier that way. She wiped her eyes, letting her jacket sleeve fall over her wrist so that she could use it like a handkerchief.

She was just too miserable to hold it in.

*I* expected to feel miserable. I hadn't wanted to come to this dance until I—well, until I did, and here I was, disappointing another girl. But the least expected and most overwhelming thing, I was grateful. Do you know what I mean? She trusted me.

I wanted to tell her.

Oh, I had about forty arguments against it. And not a single word to recommend it. Except that she needed me. All of me, Vincenzo Gold, in one piece. If she would have me.

But Vinnie Gold didn't say any of that. Didn't ask questions. Vinnie Gold might care, but he didn't offer advice on things he didn't know anything about.

"This isn't because I'm in love with him or anything," she said by way of apology. "I sent him a note telling him I didn't want to go out again. But I let him talk me into dancing with him. Bully me, really." She fought against crying harder. "I'm acting like a dope."

"Don't say that."

"It makes it worse, huh?" She started to walk away. We were nearly home. I followed her, but she started to walk faster, getting ahead of me.

I couldn't leave it at that. I didn't want to run after her, so I called, sounding irritated. "Patsy." That seemed in line with being cool.

She slowed down and we walked for a block without saying anything. She went through her pockets and came up with some tissue to blow her nose. Finally she asked, "Are you always so tough?"

"Tough?" *No, cool,* I wanted to say.

"You don't know that you're tough?" she asked, looking straight at me as we approached the streetlight on our corner. "Hard to get to?" Her manner had changed to one I was more familiar with. She was about to hang up on me.

I'd pictured her with lips compressed into a thin line, eyes snapping, electric sparks in the air around her head. It was a picture that brought a smile to my heart. But she wasn't like that at all. She looked like someone treading deep water. An expression of superficial calm, panic lurking in her eyes.

"No," I said, finally. I was really sorry I'd gone with

sounding annoyed. I could've been cool enough just by walking along until she slowed down.

She sighed and looked away, pulling the elastic bands to the ends of the ponytails. Her hair fell tousled to her shoulders. The sight of it knocked me out. It just knocked me out. I could have looked at her hair all night. "Patsy?"

"Yes?"

"I don't mean to seem tough."

She was talking to the Vinnie Gold of the dance floor. Someone who acted a lot like Vincenzo talked, someone who looked bolder and better than the Vinnie I really was.

"Hey, there's a new movie opening next week—"

She didn't meet my eyes. "I'm kind of busy next week, Vinnie."

"Okay. Some other time, maybe."

She stopped on the sidewalk in front of her house, but I kept walking, shivering a little, turning and strolling backward in a cool, casual way.

She said, "I really can't go next week. You'll ask again, right?"

"Sure, sure." Sure. "See you then." And I turned toward my house.

The old Vinnie would have stood there awkwardly, making helpless conversation while his heart bled. Vincenzo—I would've thought he wouldn't take no for an answer. Me, the one walking away as if it didn't matter whether she said yes or no—who was he?

Will the real Vinnie Gold please stand up?

# FIFTY

I paced my room for the next twenty-five minutes, seeing the whole evening in instant replay. It was hard to figure out where we'd go from here. Would I keep calling her every night at midnight? Maybe we'd meet again in the darkness.

Unless she guessed my name tonight.

Would I be truthful? Or would I do the only thing I could to preserve our relationship?

Lie.

11:58. I sat down by the phone, my foot trying to jiggle away the tension I felt. Put Vinnie Gold out of your mind, I thought. You're the midnight caller, a man of unleashed passions. I grinned. All right, it was comic relief, but the bottom line? Patsy was there for me. Right where I asked her to be. Me. The melting, bleeding, rapidly beating heart of Vincenzo Gold.

11:59. If you want to know the truth, I was suddenly wild with jealousy. She was practically salivating over Vinnie Gold on the dance floor, but still meeting me in secret, hoping I'd turn out to be—who? And then she didn't want to go to the movies, or was she playing hard to get?

I had to stop thinking. Trying to figure her out. Trying to plan. The whole thing was making me crazy. I had to see what her reaction to the evening was, and then I'd know where I stood. Maybe.

Midnight. I dialed.

Ringing.

Picked up. Nothing. Not even the sound of her breathing.

"Are you there?" I asked.

"Yes."

"Why didn't you say hello?"

"I felt funny." Her voice still held the extra layer it had in the book room, a nervous edge. Excitement. "Don't you?"

"I'm a wreck," I admitted, and felt better immediately.

"Sometimes you say exactly what I'm feeling, you know that?"

"I hear you had a falling-out with Biff." Fast on my feet.

"He has a jealous streak."

"Among other more serious tendencies."

She said, "You were right about him."

"What are you telling me?"

"There's been a kind of meanness in the way he's been treating me lately. Trying to play along, but like he's impatient to get to the end of something." I should've been loving this, but it made my skin creep. "And he's so possessive," she went on. "I thought he was going to hit me when I got back to the dance. I didn't let him bring me home."

I didn't want to get into that. "Game's over?"

"Yes."

"You shouldn't play such dangerous games," I said, wanting to be witty, urbane. But it suddenly felt too true to be that slick. "What about tonight? What do you want, anyway?"

"Want?"

"You met a stranger in a dark room tonight, Patsy."

"I met you."

"An obscene caller."

"Zorro."

My breath caught. Did this mean she knew? On the walk home? Or just since we were talking? Or was she trying to hedge her bet, choosing both Vinnie and Vincenzo?

"I guess it's not Italian," Patsy said, into what she might have perceived to be an offended or maybe bored silence. "But I want it to be tonight's name. Until you give me yours."

"I was at the dance, remember? I saw you with him."

Silence. And then she said, "Look, he's nice enough, and I loved dancing with him. But he's not the kind of guy I'm ever going to get to know. He's smooth and all, but he's not like you. He'll never say anything important."

"What do you want him to say?" My voice came out hoarse.

"I don't want him to say anything. He's a Ken doll with a ring in his back. Pull the ring and get a cute remark."

"He's safe, though. Didn't you want to say something to one of your friends? 'If I'm not back in twenty minutes, look for me in the book room?'" I knew I'd pushed for it, but now I wished I'd played things differently. "Why would you do such a crazy thing?"

"It's not crazy," she said. "You'll trust me now, right?"

"I'm saying you shouldn't have trusted *me*. How could you be sure I wasn't going to act like Biff?"

"How can you say that? After all the things we've talked about." She sounded truly shaken. But she came back fast. Mad. "You want to go on this way, don't you?"

I said, "Don't get angry."

"You get angry."

"I have a weak character."

"Don't make jokes." She made an irate sniffling noise. "It's enough for you? Whispering sweet nothings in my ear?" She was going for sarcasm, but not making it. "Don't you ever just want to hold hands?"

"I want both."

"We could have both."

I wished she was right. I hoped she was. But I couldn't quite bring myself to believe it. To believe her.

"If it's going to be that you can't take it if I'm not always thinking of ways to keep you interested," she said, "or if I'm not going to be able to face my friends with you, let's just find it out."

"So you can make up your mind about the other guy?"

"Don't be like that." She sounded outraged. Caught at playing both sides until she'd made up her mind.

"When it's over with the dancer," I said as steadily as I could manage, "it will be over." My voice was shaking like crazy. "But I'll still be here all along, talking to you. We'll be—"

"What makes you think I'll want to talk to you while I have a boyfriend? Don't you think he'd be enough for me? Do you think I'd be stringing some other guy along?"

Actually, that was exactly what I thought. Actually, I knew it. The question was, how could I tell her I knew it?

"You think I was honest with you because we're only talking on the phone," she said. "But I was open even though I don't know who you are. I was honest even though you know who I am."

"I don't think you were entirely honest."

"You're never going to tell me who you are," she said too quietly, and it was a simple statement, not a question at all.

"I don't know," I said, and it was the most truthful answer I could give her.

"Maybe you don't like girls so much after all. You found yourself a way to have one like a pet."

She was wrong. At least I hoped so.

I felt like she was driving me into a corner, and if I could just think for a minute, I'd know how to answer, how to turn the tables.

"You know what else I think?"

"Please—"

"I think you're no better than Biff," she cried, her voice mingling frustration and a desperate appeal. "You're different, that's all, you're weirder. But you're no better."

Click.

I moved the phone back to the bedside table. It was a tremendous effort. She could have had this whole conversation without me, and that's about what she did.

Probably I should have called her right back. It was possible she expected me to do just that. Maybe we would go on talking about something else, like we'd done before. She'd try to guess my name.

But somehow I knew she wouldn't try. She wouldn't even pick up. I lay in the darkness, thinking—or not thinking most of the time, feeling a dull ache, amputation pain.

Except that it was nearly painless, as feelings go; it was almost comforting. I don't think it would be right to say that I let myself drown, but I didn't fight it off.

After a time, sensation returned to my body. I could feel the smooth cotton bedspread beneath my fingers. The floor felt solid beneath my feet, reassuring as I stood and walked across my room. Testing. Everything worked. Everything felt fine now.

I looked out my window. Her room was dark.

I went back to bed.

It was what I'd been afraid of all along. I couldn't bring myself to tell her who I was. How could I? I saw how wrong

I'd been to meet her in the book room. It was erosion. Maximum entropy. Sand on the beach.

Of course she'd found Vincenzo wanting. He seemed more courageous while cowering in his room. The first thing I had to ask myself was, Was she right? Did I really want us to go on this way? No. Because didn't Vinnie have the sweeter deal? She might not tell all, but he could sit next to her when he talked to her. He could kiss her.

And there was still this shocking idea she had, that she had to take these crazy risks. Wasn't I right? Talk about weird. How come it was falling to an obscene caller to keep her from harm?

I had a funny thought just before I fell asleep.

If we were to stretch the phone wire from my bed to hers, right through the window and across the driveway, we wouldn't need thirty feet. And we were both crying ourselves to sleep tonight.

I woke up in the middle of the night. It was all resolved in my head. It felt terrible. All the clichés. Like I'd never love anyone else. Like it was the end of the world. Like this pain would never go away. I decided the thing to do, feel pretty good for Vinnie Gold, who, if he played his cards right, had himself a girl. I wouldn't die of love. Dying of love was out.

# FIFTY-ONE

The way things worked out, I ran into her as she went out for the paper the next morning. I was on the same errand, giving me a fairly uninteresting opening as we walked down our driveways. "Funny we don't run into each other this way more often."

"I'm usually out here much earlier."

"Early to bed, early to rise?"

"I go to sleep early," she said with a little shrug.

So much for truth-telling.

"I meant what I said last night. The movie? I'd like to do it again sometime."

"That's okay, Vinnie," she said. "I appreciate it. Really."

"That sounds like a no."

"You looked at me differently after you got punched out in the locker room. You were different."

She was right. But not for the reasons she thought. How could I say that Vincenzo was the one who got mad at her?

"I mean, for me it stopped being about the good time we had last Sunday," she said. "I'm embarrassed about the things he said about me."

She tucked their paper under her arm and started back for the house without me. I grabbed our paper, closer to the curb, and dashed back to her.

"Admit it," she said. "Part of the reason you keep asking is just to be nice."

"What if I took you to the movies to be nice," I said, "but I bought you the hot chocolate because I really like you?"

Wrong. It was written all over her face. Right then—not a moment before, I don't know why—but right then, I remembered what she'd said about Vinnie Gold. A Ken doll.

I tried again. "I asked you because I thought we'd have a good time again, and we did." Which was as real as Vinnie Gold could get.

I should've just tied a stone around my neck and jumped in.

Because what I wanted to tell her right then, sometimes a guy just likes the way a girl sounds late at night. And when her eyes widened, I could say, *So of course I'll keep on calling at midnight, even if I've just brought you home.* But Vincenzo had blown his last chance.

So what I said was, "I took you out because I like you, Patsy." No frills.

She gave me an odd look. I lost any points I'd gotten for

honesty, because I didn't quite meet her eyes. Telling the truth is tougher than it sounds.

"I'm not saying no to you personally, Vinnie. I don't think I'm going to go out for a while," she said. "I'm off dating."

We had reached our doors, and both of us hesitated. I was trying to get up the nerve to say the kind of thing that Vincenzo found so easy. But Patsy beat me to the punch.

"You're a good guy, I know how nice you were to me—" And then she pulled out all the stops. She used honesty. "I almost thought you were—it sounds stupid, I know, but I kept thinking you were going to turn out to be somebody else. I thought there was this soft part you were protecting—there's just nothing soft about you, Vinnie. That's not your fault, you don't have to be different for me, so I'm just sorry, okay?" she finished, in a tone that didn't sound sorry at all.

She opened her door and stood there, waiting to see if I had anything more to say. I'm not a glutton for punishment. I decided to take her at her word, at least for the moment. I opened the kitchen door and went inside without another word to her. I wish I could say Vinnie Gold ran his fingers through his hair and strolled off, the winnah. But it didn't really feel that way.

Vincenzo had been right all along. I was the one.

But in a funny way, she had said the right thing. What might have happened if I had done the same?

Real meeting real.

An underwater earthquake. Foundations being ripped

asunder miles below, and nary a ripple on the surface of the water. In a way, that's what had happened, even though only one of us knew about it.

"Vinnie," Mom said. She was sitting with Mr. B, dunking a French glazed. Mr. B had made an early-morning run to the donut shop. "Can we have the paper?"

I set it down on the table. "Hot chocolate in the mug," Mr. B said, sort of in breakfast code as the phone rang. He got up to answer it, said "Good morning, Ma."

I headed for the teapot and poured boiling water into the mug, stirring. "Hey, Mom, you remember Paul?"

"Paul who?"

"I don't know. He was your Paul."

"Oh! Of course I remember him."

Mr. B stepped into the dining room with his conversation, phone cord stretched and jiggling.

I asked Mom, "Who was he, exactly?"

"First guy to love me. First one to tell me so, anyway. What a character."

"What kind of character?" I made much of choosing from assorted donuts, hoping she'd talk.

"We grew up together, so I was aware of every silly kid thing he ever did. Awful things, sometimes. I didn't take him seriously. But I broke up with my longtime boyfriend two days before the prom, and Paul stepped in to take me to the dance. And to a dance club in the city after. And to the beach at daybreak."

She snatched up the last French glazed donut as my

hand hovered too near, and added, "We were with a whole bunch of kids, of course, but that night I learned he'd loved me through most of our teen years."

"So how come you and Dad used to sound sort of mean about him?"

"Did we?"

"Well. I was a kid. I could be wrong. But why would you say to Dad, 'Remember Paul?' And then laugh."

"Ah. Well, your dad almost didn't marry me."

!!!

I was glad I had just taken a big bite. It covered my surprise.

"About a week before the wedding, he got cold feet. And Paul offered to step in." This last bit about Paul was said with real affection. "Sometimes I wonder."

"Wonder what?"

"About Paul. He was such a great guy."

"Even though he did all those things you mentioned. Awful things?"

"Probably because of them," Mom said. "Out of all the guys I dated or even didn't date back then, he was memorable, you know?"

"Where is he now?"

"Married the prom queen and moved to Seattle, last I heard."

"The prom queen?"

"She had been, yes, but when he married her, she was a fashion buyer, moving out there to work for a big department store. And he was moving out there with her, moving his practice, way before it was fashionable to do that kind of thing."

"His practice?"

"He was a lawyer. Defending the undefendable, of course."

Mr. B came back and said to Mom, "Ma wants to say hello."

I was standing in front of my breath-fogged bedroom window around five o'clock, maybe five-thirty, looking forward to spaghetti and meatballs. It was dark, of course, but I could see a few snowflakes drifting past the window.

I saw Patsy leave by her back door. She walked down the drive, not especially fast and not particularly purposefully. I watched long enough to see which way she went, thinking it was good I had my work boots on. No time to waste.

"Vinnie, what's the rush?" Mom wanted to know as I sped through the living room. "I'm about to take the spaghetti out of the oven."

"Save some for me," I yelled back to her. "I'm going for a walk."

# FIFTY-TWO

I ran up the block, pulling on my jacket, and when I got to the corner, I could see Patsy turning onto the next block under a streetlamp. She was walking faster now, the snow still lazily blowing.

I set a pace for myself and caught up with her. She looked back and saw me coming, but she didn't react, didn't wait. "Would you mind a little company?" I asked, pulling up beside her. "It's a little late for you to be out alone."

"It isn't even six o'clock," she said, but any rejection that had been intended was muted when she sniffled.

I took that for a maybe. "It's dark," I said, and hoped that settled it. I put my hands in my pockets like I had gotten into a stride.

"I'm sorry I was mean to you today."

"You weren't—"

"Yes, I was. I was wrong, too. Everybody has soft places, including you." Sniffle, sniffle. But there were no tears when we passed beneath a streetlamp.

"Yesterday, that wouldn't have been what I wanted to hear." Too true. And it had taken me hours to hear what she'd said earlier, what she was saying now. She hadn't appreciated Vincenzo for his detachment, or Vinnie Gold for his cool. She wanted the guy with feelings on display, whoever he was.

I hesitated. I couldn't afford to get clever now. Patsy and I were mapping out fresh territory here, on dry land. She'd told me what she wanted. Someone authentic and un-guarded.

She gave me that odd look again, and this time I made myself meet it. "What about today?" she said. "Tonight?"

"I'm thinking about it." Okay, okay, it wasn't total honesty, but at least I didn't lose any points for that answer. We cut through a little path that ran between two properties. It was much darker as we crossed the backyard of an unlit house. I asked, "Are we headed anyplace special?"

"No," she said. "Okay, yes, but I'm not on an errand or anything. No one's lived here for a while, but somebody keeps up the goldfish pond. I like to come sit beside it." Then she laughed. "I guess it's a little dark to see the fish."

But we sat anyway, on a cold stone bench. Ice covered the surface of the pond. The snow ticked faintly as it landed on the ice.

"When did you come here last?" I asked her.

"In September."

"I think they've taken the fish someplace else for the winter."

"I hope so," she said. "I never came to see them in winter before. When they're in the pond, even if it's dark, you can hear them come to the surface."

"I know. The angelfish in my tank do that. Blip, blip."

"Exactly."

It was a strange feeling, being so aware of her in the darkness. Both of us so quiet I could hear her hair brush against the fabric of her jacket. I heard when she allowed her breath to leave her in a small sigh. Very much like talking to her on the phone. That surprised me.

Somehow, despite the satisfaction I'd taken in our late-night talks, I'd always felt there must be something lacking. Some sensual thrill that could only be enjoyed if I could touch her. That's what meeting her at the dance was about. And I'm not saying that touch didn't add to the experience, immeasurably. But I understood for the first time how completely we shared a real intimacy. Vincenzo had said it once, hadn't he? We could tell each other anything. We had.

"I have the strangest feeling, sitting here with you," she said. "Like we've been friends for such a long time. So different than I felt earlier today."

It was an appropriate moment, I decided, and I said, "I've had some time to think it over and it's probably easier if we aren't trying to go it alone." I could hear some deep-down shakiness in my voice, and I was sharply aware that she could hear it, too.

"What?"

"I'm talking about what you said about survival." Okay, so I was shaky, but I was on dry land. "You know. About taking risks. The other night."

"Vinnie?" Breathlessly. I think. I hoped. I was too terrified to trust my own judgment.

"Vincenzo."

"Vincenzo . . . Gold?" she said, her voice rising on "Gold."

"My father's name is Vincent, but being something of a romantic, and being married to an Italian woman, he—"

"Your mother is Italian?" Breathlessly. No mistaking.

"I'm fifty percent. Ask me if *I'm* Italian, for Pete's sake!"

"It is you."

There was a long, still moment during which I reflected that I had offered her my earth-shaking revelation. Real meeting real. And the world hadn't come to an end. It made me brave. "So you still have a craving for Italians?"

She made a little sound in the darkness, something between a cough and a sob. I didn't hesitate. I put my arm around her waist, held on to her elbow. I thought she'd started to cry.

I might cry too, it had been a hell of a day.

But she was laughing. "I knew it," she shouted. "Twice I knew it, but then you would sound so sure of yourself, arrogant, and I talked myself out of it."

"Arrogant?" I felt a smile stretch itself across my face. "Vinnie Gold is not arrogant. Vinnie Gold is suave."

What she did, she put an arm around my neck and hugged. Hard. And she was still laughing when she let go. Me, I hadn't smiled like that in years. Maybe ever.

She said, "Vincenzo?"

I loved the way she said it. "Yes?"

"How did you change your voice?"

"I put a couple of folds of T-shirt around the phone."

"No way that was all."

I shrugged. "Mostly, I just sounded more confident."

"Not really."

"No?"

"I would have guessed," she said. "Soon."

God, she was so real. One thing I finally got, if she held surprises—and of course, she would—they were going to be the kind I could handle. Knowing that made me feel so grounded.

We started back home. We stopped along the way to take a look at each other in the light. I think we both liked what we saw.

And if it gets a little scary, well, we can hold each other's hand.

# ACKNOWLEDGMENTS

The lovely thing about thanking Shana and Jill, and the copy editors and the art department at Random House, even though I have before, is that I'm still thanking them. They are the marshmallows in my hot chocolate, and I lift my cup to them. A special thank-you and an extra marshmallow to Alison Kolani and Susan Wallach.

# ABOUT THE AUTHOR

Audrey Couloumbis is the author of several highly acclaimed novels, including *Getting Near to Baby* (a Newbery Honor winner) and *War Games*, which she wrote with her husband, Akila Couloumbis. Audrey grew up in Illinois and in Queens, New York, where she attended Forest Hills High School, like Vinnie. She and Akila met when she hailed the taxi he was driving down Broadway. She currently divides her time between upstate New York and Florida.